$1.50

She didn't want to keep remembering...

But Catriona's mind refused to stop dwelling on what had happened with Peter the night before. Of course, he'd kissed her on impulse. Even men like Peter Vilhena must occasionally act impulsively, and there was no doubt that he'd regretted it immediately.

What had he said? "I'm sorry. That shouldn't have happened."

Fiercely Catriona told herself that Peter's gesture had meant nothing. He'd obviously been troubled, and though she couldn't even begin to guess what his burden was, she'd felt a tremendous uprush of sympathy...and something else. The intensity of her own feelings had shaken her.

Nevertheless, Peter would certainly have forgotten it all by now, and it was best that she do the same. But that was proving impossible....

The Sun
and Catriona

by

ROSEMARY POLLOCK

Harlequin Books

TORONTO • LONDON • LOS ANGELES • AMSTERDAM
SYDNEY • HAMBURG • PARIS • STOCKHOLM • ATHENS • TOKYO

Original hardcover edition published in 1981
by Mills & Boon Limited

ISBN 0-373-02486-X

Harlequin edition published July 1982

CHAPTER ONE

ALTHOUGH it was well past eleven o'clock, the big dining-room was still crowded. People were lingering over their coffee, talking and laughing, reluctant to move. Probably this was because outside, beyond the heavily curtained windows, it was a damp, disappointingly dreary August evening. Puddles were forming in the car park, the temperature had dropped to fifty degrees Fahrenheit, and miles of rain-sodden countryside lay between the Calverley Hotel and civilisation. It was depressing, especially for the dozen or so foreign tourists currently patronising the Calverley, but in spite of the weather it was generally felt that the place had its compensations. The trout pâté had been very good, the *escalopes de veau* even better, and the Gâteau St. Honoré was a triumph. The chef had excelled himself, and several diners were sending him congratulatory messages. The Calverley had an international reputation for comfort, cuisine and service, and though its patrons tended to expect rather a lot they were not usually disappointed.

Cautiously, Catriona allowed herself to lean for a moment against the wall beside the kitchen door. Waitresses weren't supposed to lean against anything, but her feet were tired and swollen and there was a steady, nagging pain in her back, which seemed to be in danger of splitting. The hotel was unusually full and she had been on duty for five hours without a break. She was glad, tonight, that her stint as a waitress had only another four weeks to run. For a summer job it wasn't bad. The pay was good and she had plenty of free time, which was important, but there were occasions when she could wish she had picked a slightly less exhausting method of earning essential cash. She longed to sit down for a moment, but knew that even if she had been allowed to do anything so revolutionary she might have found it difficult to stand up again. She glanced around the room, watching hopefully for signs of movement. The American couple by the door caught her eye, but—no, they weren't moving, they were signalling. With an effort she threaded her way between the tables, summoning a determined smile.

'Do you think we could have some more coffee?'

They sounded mildly apologetic, and although she was beginning to feel a trifle weary, Catriona warmed towards them. She replenished their cups, and as she did so became aware of the fact that someone else was trying to attract her attention.

It was the man at the next table, and deliberately she avoided his eye. She didn't usually take unreasoning dislikes to people—and as far as the hotel's patrons were concerned she did her best to like them —but this particular guest had been rather difficult. He was autocratic, for one thing, and he rarely appeared to be satisfied—with the hotel, the service, or even with the menu. He didn't say much, but his manner was abrupt, and although he hadn't actually been rude to Catriona he frequently gave the impression that he was having difficulty in controlling his temper. It was absurd, for as far as she knew the Calverley Hotel had given him no reasonable cause for complaint, and he hadn't any right to be difficult. If he had been an older man, or some sort of invalid, she would have made allowances. But he wasn't much more than thirty, his health was obviously excellent, and there was no doubt at all that he was wealthy. She had no time for him whatsoever. Unlike Kathy, the junior receptionist, who had been bowled over—by one glance from a pair of brilliant dark eyes, she was quite unimpressed by the fact that he was so good-looking, and his faint, elusive accent had also failed to captivate her. She knew that he came from an island in the Mediterranean and bore an unusual title—The Most Noble Count Vilhena— but she had no desire to discover more than that. She simply saw him as the kind of thing that made her job unnecessarily tiresome, and if she had needed further excuses for disliking him they had been provided during the last hour or so.

Tonight he had a young girl with him, and as soon as they entered the dining-room it had been obvious that they were related to one another. The girl was pretty, but although her features were softer, she bore a very noticeable resemblance to the man sharing her table. They had the same glossy black hair, the same slanting eyebrows, the same prominent cheekbones. Eventually it emerged that they were brother and sister, and it wasn't very long before Catriona found herself feeling sorry for the girl. Her brother was apparently in an even more impatient mood than usual, making no attempt whatsoever to conceal the fact. When his sister hesitated over the menu, his fingers drummed impatiently on the tablecloth, and when she finally came to a decision, he criticised her choice. At other times he barely spoke to her.

As far as Catriona was concerned, he could have waited for his coffee, or his liqueur, or whatever it was he wanted. But he was a guest, and it was her duty to see that his needs were attended to. When she had made certain that the American couple wanted nothing further, she turned to him.

'Yes, sir?'

He barely looked up. 'More coffee, please.'

She fetched the coffee-pot and began to refill his sister's cup. As she did so, the girl smiled at her.

'You must be so tired.' Her accent was more noticeable than her brother's, but she sounded pleasant.

'Just a bit,' Catriona admitted.

'When do you stop working?'

'When everyone stops eating. Perhaps twelve o'clock.'

'Oh! That's very late. When do you start?'

'Usually at half past six. We have to make sure everything is ready.'

'But that's terrible! Peter, don't you think so?'

Her brother shrugged. Catriona turned to replenish his cup, and as she did so she stumbled, losing her balance for a moment. The coffee-pot slipped in her grasp, and before she could do anything to prevent it a torrent of hot black coffee cascaded from the spout. Paralysed with horror, she watched as it splashed down on to the immaculate sleeve of the guest's dinner-jacket.

'I-I'm sorry!' she gasped. Gaining control of the coffee-pot, she set it down on the table while slowly a dark stain began to spread across the snowy cloth.

People at other tables were turning to stare, and for a second or so the dark girl sat motionless, as if she had witnessed an act of sacrilege. Then she stifled a giggle. Her brother removed his dinner-jacket, revealing the fact that the coffee had already begun to seep through.

'Has it—has it burnt your arm?' Catriona asked apprehensively.

'No.' He stood up, frustrating her efforts to mop his sleeve with a napkin. 'You may be tired,' he remarked coldly, eyeing her with dislike, 'but I'm sure you're adequately paid, and in your position I would try to be a little less clumsy. If I were your employer, I would not tolerate carelessness.'

His sister's eyes opened very wide. 'She could not help it—she tripped!'

Catriona stood still, the napkin in her hand. It annoyed her to find that her fingers were trembling. She knew that at this point she should apologise profusely, fetch more coffee, and then take the irate guest's jacket from him, making a soothing promise to have it in the hands of the dry cleaning department by eight o'clock the following morning. After that, she realised, she ought to change the tablecloth, sponge the carpet, and inform the head waiter that there had been a slight accident.

She knew exactly what she ought to do, and for at least a minute she really meant to go through with it. Then she looked up into the dark face of the man who had been addressed as Peter, and something seemed to snap inside her.

'I have apologised,' she reminded him, 'and I'm perfectly willing to apologise again. I'm sorry about your jacket, and if it's damaged I'll—I'll pay for a replacement.' As she spoke, the thought ran through her mind that his jacket was probably worth more than she was likely to earn in a fortnight, but that couldn't be helped. Her breath coming rapidly, she ploughed on. 'I'm sorry if I've spoilt your evening. It was an accident, though you probably won't believe that. But I won't apologise for existing, and I won't let anyone talk to me as if I were—as if I were a Roman slave-girl! Since I started work in this hotel I've met all sorts of people, and most of them have been very nice, but—but just occasionally there's someone like you, and it makes me angry. You value your comfort, but you don't even notice the people who work hard to provide it for you. You like life to run smoothly, but when someone tries to make sure that it does you can't even spare the time to say thank you. You're impossible! You're—you're a parasite!'

She stopped, aware that a deadly silence had fallen in the dining-room. A firm hand touched her arm, and she saw that the manager was standing beside her.

'You've said quite enough, Catriona. Go to my office. I'll deal with you in a few minutes.' He turned away from her and began making apologetic noises in the direction of his affronted guest. He was, as she had always realised, very good at his job. She left the room quickly, only partially conscious of the aston-ished stares that followed her to the door. As she vanished from view she knew that a murmur of com-ment broke out behind her, and she walked faster still, almost running down the beige-carpeted corri-dor that led towards the front of the hotel.

In the manager's office it was quiet and still. Lucy,

Mr Denning's secretary, had finished work hours before and her desk was tidy. There was a grey carpet and a wall lined with grey filing-cabinets; a bookshelf crammed with guidebooks, gazetteers, hotel lists and trade directories. On the manager's huge maplewood desk a massive ledger lay open, and three jade-green telephones clustered together as if for mutual protection.

Catriona shivered and sat down. Despite the fact that the central heating was operating very efficiently, she felt cold. In some ways she didn't regret what she had done. She had said what needed to be said. But she was sorry to have let Mr Denning down. He had been a fair and reasonable employer.

A minute or two later Mr Denning came into the room. She saw at once that he wasn't looking forward to the interview in front of him, and she braced herself, lifting her chin.

'Well, Catriona.' Going round behind his desk, he sat down and cleared his throat. When she said nothing, he glanced at her. 'I've apologised to Count Vilhena. Fortunately, he doesn't seem to have paid much attention to your outburst. You knew who he was, I suppose?'

She shook her head. 'I only knew that he had some sort of outlandish title—The Most Noble Count Vilhena.' Swiftly she added: 'I'm sorry, Mr Denning. I didn't mean to behave so badly. But—but I was tired tonight. And he's not a very pleasant person.'

The manager leant back in his chair. 'You did pour a pot of coffee over his dinner-jacket.'

'I know, but it wasn't just that. He's been so difficult—ever since he arrived.'

'I see. You thought this particular guest was difficult. So, in a crowded dining-room, you told him what you thought of him.'

Recognising the ominous note in his voice, she tilted her head defensively. 'I'm sorry, but I couldn't help it.'

'Well, that's fair enough. You've been straightforward with me, and now I must be straightforward with you. I can't keep you on, Catriona. I know your ambition is to paint pictures, and you only took this job as a way of making ends meet, but I can't tolerate artistic temperament in a member of my staff. Not when it means allowing you to insult a Maltese millionaire who could easily, if he likes us, become a very valuable customer.' He cleared his throat a second time. 'I'm sorry, but it might happen again, and I can't take the risk.'

Catriona stood up. 'I understand.'

'Well, I hope you do.' He looked mildly uncomfortable. 'You were to have been with us for another four weeks and of course you will be paid for that length of time, but I must ask you not to do any more work. In the morning my secretary will give you a cheque, and you may keep your room here until you've found another job.'

Catriona had a lot of pride, inherited, like her temper, from a redheaded Highland grandmother, and she longed for the strength of will to refuse his offer of payment which was not going to be earned. But she couldn't afford to refuse it. This summer's earnings were going to have to keep her through the winter that lay ahead. During the winter she would hibernate, living very cheaply, and while she was hibernating she would paint. So that by next spring she would be ready for her Exhibition.

As she turned to leave the room, Mr Denning nodded to her. 'Goodnight, Catriona.'

'Goodnight, Mr Denning.' Behind her, the office door clicked shut, and she walked slowly away towards the lift reserved for staff.

CHAPTER TWO

BACK in her small, neat room on the third floor, Catriona sat in front of the dressing-table mirror, staring thoughtfully at her own reflection. She saw clear grey eyes, a fair, unblemished skin, medium-length brown hair. She wasn't a beauty, she knew that, but people seemed to think she was reasonably pretty, and she had always taken care of her appearance. Maybe she could get a job as a receptionist—that would help. She had always known she would need to go on working for a week or so after her term ended at the Calverley.

She hadn't expected this, though.

Slowly she unpinned the crisp white cap that was still firmly attached to her hair, and placing it in a drawer attempted to sort out her thoughts. She didn't regret losing her temper. For a moment, as she gazed into the mirror, the Maltese Count's dark face seemed to hover in front of her, and she felt again a wild surge of resentment. The Most Noble Count Vilhena . . . *Noble?* Catriona could think of a different word. He was the most insufferable kind of human being. She had had to let him know how she felt. She couldn't possibly have reacted in any other way.

But it was a pity, just the same. She had been fond of the Calverley Hotel.

Just as she was about to take her apron off, someone knocked lightly on her bedroom door, and she paused, biting her lip. It was bound to be one of the other girls from the dining-room, probably come to offer sympathy, and she wasn't sure that she could cope with sympathy. Not just at the moment. She liked Sandy, and she liked Vanessa, but she had seen their shocked faces as she left the dining-room, and she knew there was no way they would be able to understand.

Wearily she called: 'Come in.'

The door opened. Still struggling with the tie of her apron, Catriona glanced up casually. Then she stiffened, for the girl standing in the doorway wasn't Sandy or Vanessa, or anyone connected with the staff of the hotel. She was tall, slim and very dark.

She was the sister of the Maltese Count.

'I'm so sorry. Did I startle you?' Her accent was very noticeable. She obviously felt unsure of herself.

For several seconds Catriona stared, as if she had seen an apparition. Then she made an effort to pull herself together. She couldn't imagine why this girl had come to see her, but the situation had to be handled somehow.

'It's all right,' she said quietly. 'Come in. Is there —is there something I can do for you?'

The girl closed the door behind her and advanced into the room. Standing by the dressing-table, she looked around.

'It's very small,' she said. 'This room.'

Catriona said nothing, and the girl smiled at her. She really was extraordinarily pretty.

'I am being rude,' she said. 'I didn't mean to be. Are you sad because you are leaving?'

Catriona felt taken aback. 'How do you know I'm leaving?' she asked.

'I asked the manager.' The Maltese girl lifted a silver-backed hairbrush from Catriona's dressing-table. 'But you have some pretty things!' She fingered the silver lovingly. 'This is beautiful. Someone gave it to you?'

'My mother.' Putting out a hand, Catriona took the brush from her. 'Look, Miss—Miss Vilhena. . . .'

'I'm not Miss Vilhena, I'm Toni Caruana. Peter is my half-brother.'

'Oh. Well, Miss Caruana, I'm a little bit tired, and I'd like to go to bed. I'm sorry about your brother's jacket, as I told him downstairs, but at least you can now let him know that justice is being done.'

Toni Caruana gazed at her for a moment, and then she laughed. 'Peter doesn't care about his jacket. Or about you. He was just in a temper to-night, and you got in his way.'

'I see.' Several acid comments sprang to Catriona's lips, but she stifled them. 'Well, thank you for telling me.'

'I didn't come to tell you that.' Without bothering to ask permission the Maltese girl sat down on Catriona's bed. 'I came to offer you a job.'

Catriona gave her a quick look.

'You . . . what did you say?'

'I'm offering you a job. Peter knows about it, and he thinks it's a good idea. Not that I'd care if he didn't.' A defiant look appeared in the dark eyes. 'Peter doesn't own me. He isn't even my guardian—not while Papa is still alive.'

Following the example of her uninvited guest, Catriona sat down.

'I don't think I understand,' she said slowly.

'Oh! Perhaps I don't explain things very well.

They used to say that at school.' She gestured expressively. 'I shall begin at the beginning. My name is Antoinette Caruana, and I am the daughter of Paul Caruana, who is an archaeologist. You have heard of him?'

Catriona murmured something polite.

'You must have heard of him. He is famous, not only in Malta. For the last two years he has been in Africa, looking for the city of Ophir.'

'That sounds interesting. What about your mother—is she in Africa too?'

'No, my mother is dead. She died when I was little.'

'I'm sorry,' Catriona said quickly.

'It is not necessary to be sorry. I don't remember her. Papa was her second husband. Before she married him she was the Countess Vilhena, and . . . and Peter is her son. Apart from Papa, he is my only relative, so while Papa is in Africa he is responsible for me.'

Catriona digested this piece of information. 'Is that very bad?' she enquired sympathetically.

Toni Caruana shrugged. 'We don't really know one another. When I was little I travelled round with my parents, and since Mama died I've been at school, at Brierley Hall. I used to see him sometimes, during the holidays, but he never took much notice of me. The trouble is that I'm eighteen now, and I left school a month ago. I've been staying with friends, not very far from here, but—but now I have to go to Malta, with Peter. My father wishes it.'

'Do you wish it?' Catriona asked.

'Perhaps—I think I'd rather stay in England, but

it could be fun. If it were not for Peter.' She hesitated, pleating Catriona's cotton bedspread between slender fingers. 'Peter doesn't want responsibilities over me, and I don't blame him really. Why should he be burdened with me?'

'Why shouldn't he?' Catriona returned crisply. 'What does his wife think about it?'

'He's not married, and of course that makes it difficult.' She looked up, apparently bracing herself. 'That's where you come in,' she announced.

'Where I come in?'

'Yes.' The words came quickly, tumbling over one another. 'Don't be offended, but you have lost your job, haven't you? And you lost it because of Peter, so he ought to make it up to you. We're leaving for Malta tomorrow, and I—Peter thinks I should have a companion.' She stopped. Suddenly she looked young and frightened. 'I think so to. I don't want to be alone out there.'

'You won't be alone. You'll have your brother, and you'll soon make friends.'

The girl's eyes widened. 'But Peter isn't—you don't know him. I couldn't talk to him, ever. And I've never lived in Malta before. I'm used to England, and English people. Besides, it's so far away.'

'It's your own country,' Catriona reminded her, a little more gently. 'I time, I expect you'll come to love it. Anyway, I couldn't go with you. I don't think your brother should be expected to employ me, and even if he were prepared to, I wouldn't want to go. I have plans, you see.' She smiled, hoping she hadn't sounded too abrupt. The other girl was eighteen, and she was twenty-two, but she felt as if they were separated by something like thirty years.

Toni Caruana wrinkled her brows. 'You don't understand. Peter has agreed that I may ask you to go with me. It is a great relief to him.'

'Apart from the fact that I was rude to him to-night, he knows nothing whatsoever about me, so I don't see how it could be any sort of relief to him.' Catriona smiled again. 'I might be the most dreadful influence. I might have all kinds of undesirable tendencies!'

'Oh, no,' the Maltese girl assured her earnestly. 'He asked the hotel manager about you.'

'Oh, he did, did he?' Catriona felt a fresh upsurge of annoyance. She was sorry for the apprehensive schoolgirl in front of her, but this whole thing was getting out of hand. She had no intention of accepting any sort of job overseas, and even if she had felt quite differently, nothing could have induced her to enter the employment of Count Vilhena. It was possible, she supposed, that for the sake of convenience he might be prepared to accept almost any kind of companion for his young half-sister, whom he seemed to regard as an undesirable burden. It was even possible, though unlikely, that he felt he should recompense Catriona herself for the fact that she had been dismissed by the Calverley Hotel.

But whatever his reasons, there was no way she could even contemplate accepting such an offer.

'I'm sorry,' she repeated. 'As I told you, I have plans.'

'What sort of plans?'

'Well . . . I'm an artist, or I hope I am. I've been through the Royal College of Art, and now I just have to get on with some serious painting. Of course, I need to make money—that's why I take jobs like this one. But during the winter I'm simply going to paint.' She hesitated, then added: 'There's someone who is prepared to give me an exhibition. But I have to produce a lot of pictures, and they must be as good as I can make them.'

The Maltese girl spread her hands in an expressive gesture. 'But in Malta you could paint many pictures.'

'Well, perhaps I could. But I might not be able to. I don't suppose your brother would want me to set up a studio in his house, and anyway, I'd naturally have some duties to think about. I wouldn't be free to paint.'

'But you would! I would not disturb you!'

Catriona was silent for a moment, then she stood up.

'Look,' she said quietly, 'I don't know why you picked on me tonight, but I suspect it was partly because you suddenly felt panicky, and there was no one else.' She added, rather stiffly: 'You may even have felt sorry for me, because I was losing my job Well, I hope you realise now that you don't need to. I have a lot to think about, and—and a lot to look forward to. As for you—well, there are plenty of agencies. They'll find someone.'

Toni Caruana got to her feet, her face dejected. 'You won't come?'

'No. I'm sorry. But I hope you have a good journey, and I'm sure you'll soon come to like Malta, if you give it a chance.'

The other girl bit her lip. 'I'm sorry I bothered you. You must be very tired.' A little awkwardly, she retreated to the door. Pausing with her hand on the door-handle, she said: 'I wish you would change your mind. I don't expect you will—but if you do, we shall be here until eleven o'clock in the morning. Our plane leaves Heathrow at half past twelve.'

Then she was gone, and Catriona drew a breath of relief.

Slowly and thoughtfully, she undressed and got into bed. She wasn't going to sit up any longer, brooding pointlessly; there would be time enough for that when the morning came. It had been a crazy, mixed-up evening, and at the moment she was too tired to get things into any sort of perspective. During the last few hours she had lost one job and refused the offer of another. Perhaps she had been wrong, but there had been no alternative, in either case.

All the same, as she drifted into sleep the thought crossed her mind that it might have been nice—it just might have been nice if she had been leaving for Malta in the morning.

Seven or eight hours later she awoke to overcast skies, a blinding headache, and a vague feeling that everything wasn't as it should be. Hastily she swung herself out of bed, and as she did so memory came back with a rush. Feeling slightly stunned, she slipped into a dressing-gown and sat down again on the bed. If it had been any other day, she would have had rather less than twenty minutes in which to take a shower, dress, and present herself for duty in the dining-room. But this morning she would not be presenting herself for duty. She could never again work in the dining-room of the Calverley Hotel.

When she was dressed, she decided that it might be better if she even skipped her usual routine of snatching a coffee in the staff canteen. She still didn't feel like coping with other members of the staff. Whether they were sympathetic or disapproving, their reactions would be equally hard to take, and anyway, she wanted to be by herself. So far it wasn't raining, so she could walk down the drive to the main gates, catch a bus into Frensham, and purchase a copy of the local newspaper. In the popular bow-fronted establishment known as Vicky's Cornerhouse she would be able to study the Situations Vacant in peace.

Overnight parking in the hotel's gravelled forecourt was not usually allowed, and since most of the guests were either asleep or in the middle of breakfast it was still almost empty when Catriona set out. But a large grey Bentley was already parked near the foot of the main entrance steps and its uniformed driver was talking to someone. As Catriona came hurrying round the side of the building she didn't notice, immediately, who the other person was, but her footsteps were crisply audible as they cut through the early morning stillness, and the man turned his head. At the same moment she glanced casually at him, then faltered slightly as she recognised the tall, elegant figure of the Maltese Count.

Bother the man! Did he have to be everywhere? Bending her head a little, she hurried past, and then almost jumped out of her skin as she realised that he was speaking to her.

'Miss Browne!'

She stood still, looking round at him. There was no doubt that he was good-looking, and in the clear morning light, dressed in English tweeds and with his dark hair immaculately brushed, he was quite a striking figure. But he didn't impress her. She wished he had had the tact to leave her alone.

After hesitating for nearly half a minute, she turned and walked a few paces towards him.

'Good morning. Did you want to speak to me?'

'Yes. May I ask you to wait a moment?' Coolly and deliberately, he finished his conversation with his chauffeur, and only when the man had climbed back behind the Bentley's steering-wheel did he turn his attention to Catriona.

'You are going for a walk?' he enquired.

'No. I'm going into Frensham. It's a town about five miles away.'

'May I ask why?'

She couldn't see why she should have to answer him, but she decided to tell the truth. 'I need to look for another job, and I might as well start now.'

He frowned. 'I understood that my sister was going to speak to you last night. If she did, you have already been offered a job.'

There was a short silence.

'Yes,' Catriona acknowledged evenly, 'your sister did speak to me, and she told me that you were . . . were prepared to offer me some kind of employment. Unfortunately, though, I'm not free to take anything but a temporary job.'

His eyebrows shot up. 'Not free? Why not?'

'It would interfere with my work. My real work, that is. I'm an artist, and I have to spend this winter preparing for an exhibition.'

He looked at her impatiently. 'The world is full of artists, Miss Browne. When and where is your exhibition to be held?'

'It's being put on by a London gallery,' she told him reluctantly. 'At the end of April.' Once again, pride compelled her to be completely honest, and she added: 'It isn't an important gallery. It isn't in a particularly good area either, but it's a marvellous start, for me. I've just got to work very hard to prepare for it—and naturally I wouldn't be able to do that if I took a job that might keep me occupied right through the winter.'

The Count glanced at his watch. She sensed that he was getting annoyed, but for reasons of his own was making an effort to control his annoyance.

'Miss Browne,' he told her crisply, 'I haven't very much time. In fact, within three hours from now I shall be leaving for Heathrow Airport. My sister will be going with me, and I would very much prefer it if she had another woman to accompany her. I have a fairly comfortable home, but it is not geared to the accommodation of solitary young women, and I shall not undertake to keep her amused. She will be bored and lonely, perhaps extremely unhappy. It did not occur to me to consider the situation until late yesterday afternoon, when she arrived to join me here, and by that time it was much too late to make arrangements in the normal way. Thanks to your uninhibited temper, which, though undesirable, does not much matter in the circumstances, you have suddenly become available, and I have no doubt that you would make Antoinette an excellent companion. I would pay you a good salary, and you would be able to devote fifty per cent of your time to the pursuit of artistic inspiration.' He paused. 'My island, Miss Browne, is famous for the quality of its light, and for the colour and translucence of its surrounding seas. Artists, I believe, have congregated there for centuries, and I am certain that your London friends would advise you not on any account to miss such an opportunity.'

Catriona stared at him. She felt temporarily at a loss. 'But. . . .' she began.

'Yes?'

'It is a long way away. And besides. . . .'

She heard the sharp intake of breath that betrayed his mounting irritation. 'You would prefer,' he suggested, 'not to work for me?'

'Don't you think,' she said candidly, 'it would be rather embarrassing for us both?'

His eyebrows ascended again. 'No,' he replied. 'Not unless you are remarkably small-minded. It is true that you have lost one job because of your attitude to me, but I am offering you something very much better, and the arrangement would be to our mutual advantage. In any case, we would see very little of one another. I lead a busy life, and shall not be spending much time with Antoinette.'

Catriona felt as if the world were in danger of turning upside down. She had lived with her plans for months now, and she had worked so hard for them. She had been so sure that she knew what she had to do. But now . . . she wasn't sure any more. If she went to Malta, she would have an opportunity to reproduce on canvas the life and colour of a Mediterranean island, and that was something she had always wanted to do. Besides, it would be wonderful, really, if she could spend this important winter in a warm and sunny climate. She seemed to see the anxious face of the forlorn Antoinette. And suddenly, so suddenly that she astonished herself, she made up her mind.

'All right,' she said slowly, 'I'll go with you. With

your sister, I mean.'

There was a tiny silence. Afterwards, she could have sworn that just for an instant relief flickered in his face, followed by something very much like surprise. But it was only a fleeting impression, and within seconds it had gone.

'Good!' he said briskly. 'I take it you have a passport?'

She nodded. 'I went to Amsterdam five years ago. My passport is still valid.'

She felt he was surprised to hear that she had not been abroad for five years. In his world, obviously, nobody stayed that long in one country. But he didn't comment. While they were talking, the clouds overhead had steadily become heavier and more threatening and now scattered drops of rain were beginning to fall, glistening on the grey body of the Bentley and on the sleeves of Catriona's jacket. He glanced upwards at the sky.

'I see that your English summer is about to catch up with us again. You had better go to your room and pack, and I suggest that you also think seriously about any arrangements you may wish to make before leaving the country. We have a little less than three hours. I shall see you, I hope, at eleven o'clock.'

Without pausing to find out whether she intended to accompany him, he strode away up the steps, and his tall figure vanished through the swing doors of the Calverley Hotel.

CHAPTER THREE

THREE hours later, having packed a couple of suit-cases and made her brief farewells, Catriona settled herself on the back seat of the Bentley. Breathlessly relieved and excited, Toni Caruana scrambled in beside her, bringing with her a cloud of light French perfume, and the English girl reflected ruefully that no one could possibly fail to recognise the enormous difference between Toni's circumstances and her own. Catriona's blue denim skirt and white shirt blouse were three years old and looked it. Her battered shoulder-bag and low-heeled sandals had been acquired during art college days. Normally, her appearance didn't worry her too much, but all at once, today, she felt shabby and dull.

Tony was beautifully made up, and she was wear-ing a light green dress that did things for her creamy southern skin. Despite the fact that she was only eighteen her figure was voluptuous, and the skilfully cut dress did nothing to minimise her curves. Not surprisingly, a bevy of porters seemed to have been vying for the privilege of carrying her luggage from the hotel. Her pigskin beauty-box was handed to her with loving solicitude. Mildly amused, Catriona found herself wondering what it would be like to possess so much blatant sex appeal, then she pushed the thought from her mind. She had enough to worry about already.

Count Vilhena established himself in the front

passenger seat, almost immediately opening a brief-
case full of papers. Obviously, he had absorbing
work to do. Once the car had drawn away from the
hotel steps and had begun gathering speed along the
broad, mile-long drive, he hardly spared a glance for
the two girls in the back.

As they sped through the dripping lanes and along
crowded motorways, en route for Heathrow Airport,
Toni chattered a good deal, and she was obviously in
high spirits because Catriona had finally decided to
accompany her. But there was no doubt that she was
inhibited by the presence of her half-brother. She
talked very little about herself or her own past life.

Catriona, sitting quietly in her corner, stared
through a wide expanse of window at the tired
August countryside flashing past them. She was leaving England, and it all seemed so strange. What a lot
of things could happen, sometimes, in just a few
short hours. Every so often her attention was drawn
back to the arrogant profile of her new employer, and
once or twice she half expected him to turn round and
say something, but he never lifted his eyes from the
documents in front of him. Whatever his business
interests were, they were evidently of paramount
importance. She was sure, still, that he was a cold-
blooded, unpleasant man, and in some ways she felt
very uneasy about the decision she had taken.

They reached the huge, sprawling airport just
before twelve o'clock and having been decanted at
Terminal One made their way into the booking hall.
Though not noisy it was very crowded. There was a
feeling of bustle, spiced with suppressed excitement.
Here, after all, one took off for the Rest of the World.
Here, anything was possible.

Within minutes their baggage had been weighed. Moving smoothly through passport and security checks, they reached the peaceful oasis of the First Class departure lounge with a quarter of an hour to wait before boarding their airliner. The Count seated himself with a copy of *Time* magazine, while Catriona joined his sister in front of the huge window overlooking the runways.

'Would I be safe to offer you a cup of coffee, Miss Browne?'

Catriona swung round quickly to see the Count holding two cups of coffee for Toni and herself. Was it her imagination or did she see a glint of humour in his eyes, as she took the cup?

The Malta flight was soon called, and within a few minutes she was climbing the short gangway that led to the Trident's First Class cabin. A smiling stewardess showed them to their places, and she found herself sitting by a starboard window, next to Toni.

'I don't like window seats,' the Maltese girl told her. 'Anyway, I've seen it all before.' She was beginning to look happier and more relaxed, almost as if she might be prepared to enjoy herself, and Catriona felt relieved. The Count had a window seat on the opposite side of the plane, and they were to be separated from him by an extremely fat Italian businessman, a circumstance which seemed to work wonders for Toni's morale. By the time they were airborne she had kicked off her shoes, retouched her make-up and piled her thick black hair on top of her head, securing it deftly with pins extracted from her beauty-box. When the steward appeared she asked for Campari and lime, then curled up in her seat like a kitten.

Sipping a tonic water, Catriona eyed her curiously. 'You must know Malta very well,' she remarked.

Toni wrinkled her nose. 'I suppose so. It's not bad, really, and it can be fun.' She hesitated. 'There was a boy, two years ago . . . someone I liked. One evening he was allowed to take me to a concert.'

Catriona smiled. 'One concert? Was that all?'

'I was only sixteen,' Toni reminded her. 'And I am Maltese. Maltese girls are not always permitted to behave like English girls—not even nowadays.' She sighed. 'But he was very nice, and now I expect he has lots of girl-friends. Perhaps he is even married.' Abstractedly, she studied her polished fingertips. 'I cannot believe, sometimes, that I am old enough to be married . . . I don't feel old enough. And yet I think it would be nice to be someone's wife.'

'Marriage is a serious thing,' Catriona pointed out. 'And I'd say you were a bit young to start worrying about it.'

'Still, it must be wonderful when there is someone who belongs only to you.'

'I'm sure it is,' Catriona agreed. 'If the "someone" is right for you.'

While lunch was being served they passed over rows of snow-capped Alps, and a short time later the Mediterranean appeared beneath them. As the plane banked a little, turning eastwards, Catriona saw that the sea was dark purple, and as smooth as glass. She had never been so far south before—Paris and Amsterdam had marked the limits of her previous travels—and she was startled by the intensity of colour. It was a shock to her senses, and she found herself longing for a paintbrush.

But when, half an hour later, they came in sight of

Malta, she felt a sharp pang of disappointment. The island was yellow-brown and rocky, scorched by sun. Dusty villages were scattered among the hills and across the arid plains, but there was no hint of vegetation or even of colour. The plane was getting lower, coming in to land, and the harsh brown landscape rushed up to meet them.

Fastening her seat-belt, Toni yawned. 'Well, here we are.'

They were down, bumping across the tarmac, and low white buildings were flashing past them. Several times they circled the small airfield, then gradually they slackened speed, coming to rest at last in front of the terminal building.

Catriona was not prepared for the searing heat that met her as she left the plane. She had tried to imagine, sometimes, what it might be like to live in a hot climate, but it had never occurred to her that air could be so stifling, or that warmth could be a tangible thing.

Immigration and Customs were dealt with swiftly, and within a short time they had moved through the booking hall and out once again into blinding sunlight. In front of the terminal building there were a few scattered palm trees and a vast car park, but some taxis and private cars were waiting close to the building itself. The Count strode ahead making straight for a gleaming white Citroën that was parked directly in front of the entrance. Catriona thought of the stately grey Bentley they had left behind in England, not to mention the chauffeur, who had also been left behind, and she wondered how many cars he possessed.

An elderly, grey-haired Maltese was waiting

beside the Citroën, and at sight of Count Vilhena he
hurried forward.

'That's Mario,' Toni informed her companion, as
they pushed their way through the crowd. 'He has
been with my family since before Peter was born. He
knows everything there is to know. I think perhaps
he is the only person Peter trusts.'

It was a relief to get into the car, away from the
violence of the sun, and as Catriona leant back she
wondered for the first time exactly where they were
going. What sort of life did Peter Vilhena lead on this
dry and dusty island? What kind of house did he
own? So far, Toni hadn't told her much, and she
hadn't particularly wanted to ask, but now she was
beginning to feel curious. Despite the heat, and the
slight disappointment she had experienced when she
first caught sight of Malta, she was looking forward to
seeing Peter Vilhena on his own home ground. Quite
possibly, she decided, he would be even more dicta-
torial there than he had been in England.

Slipping between the airport gates, they turned
into a dusty highway. Oleander bushes lined the
road, and spicy flower scents drifted through the car
windows. It was intensely hot, Catriona found herself beginning to perspire. The road ran past
churches and factories, patches of rough open ground
and rows of neat houses. These were the drab envi-
rons of the airport, reminiscent of similar areas all over
the world, but the district wasn't entirely unattract-
ive and she realised that it had a character of its own.
Some of the houses were very modern, others much
older, but they were all built of the same honey-
coloured stone, and they looked as if they regularly
absorbed the golden rays of the sun. Here and there

she glimpsed gardens, and in some of the gardens there were unexpected splashes of vivid colour. She recognised hibiscus and purple bougainvillaea, plumbago and japonica, and she wondered why, from the plane, it had all looked so lifeless.

'I didn't realise there would be so many gardens,' she said to Toni. 'From the air everything looked so burnt-up.'

'The sun is hard on us, Miss Browne. But we have many gardens, many fine old houses. Malta is a beautiful island.'

The Count had spoken without looking round. Startled by his sudden intervention, Catriona stared at the back of his head.

'I'm sure it is,' she said quietly.

'I know you'll like it,' Toni put in quickly. 'There's so much that you'll want to paint. I can't wait for you to see Peter's house. It looks right out across the sea. . . .'

'We are not going to Gozo.' This time her brother's voice had a sharp edge to it.

'Not . . .' Toni looked taken aback. 'Why not? We can't stay in Valletta, it's too hot.'

'I am extremely busy at the moment. I have a number of business appointments, and I shall be spending a great deal of time in Merchant Street.' His voice seemed to grate. 'At this time of year the temperature in Valletta is no more oppressive than it is in any other part of the Maltese Islands.'

Toni gasped. 'It will be stifling!'

'That is nonsense. You must not listen to Antoinette, Miss Browne. My house is perfectly comfortable, in winter and in summer.'

Uncertain what response was expected of her,

Catriona said nothing. Toni made an expressive face and sighed dramatically, but significantly she didn't attempt to protest further.

Ten minutes later they crossed a wide, open piazza, circled a massive central fountain, and plunged through an archway into a maze of ancient streets.

'Well, we're nearly there,' Toni said resignedly.

They were moving through streets so narrow that in some places the car seemed to be in danger of being scraped by the walls, and on either side of them tall stone buildings rose towards the sky. Catriona leant forward eagerly. So this was Valletta. From this city, for hundreds of years, the Knights of St. John had ruled Malta, at the same time keeping a benevolent eye on the whole of the Mediterranean. They passed rows of smart shops, a hotel, a consulate. Then they turned into another street, this time lined with magnificent baroque buildings. There were tall windows protected by iron grilles, coats of arms out into the stonework above massive doorways and strange, enclosed wooden balconies. Then there were narrow archways through which she caught tantalising glimpses of secret courtyards ablaze with colour. Between the houses, long, narrow flights of steps plunged downwards towards the sea.

Catriona caught her breath. It was a strange, fairy-tale city, an enchanted place.

'It's so beautiful,' she said softly.

'You think so?' Toni grimaced. 'It's very old, and some of the houses are damp. Valletta is built on a peninsula. The sea almost surrounds it.'

They turned another corner, crawled forward a few more yards, and then the car stopped. Catriona realised that they had reached their destination. A great stone house loomed over them, and to her it looked larger and more impressive than anything they had so far seen. Its baroque façade seemed to be about a hundred yards long, and it was obviously very well maintained. A long line of beautifully wrought grilles obscured the ground floor windows, and the doors were like the doors of a fortress. She was reminded, for a moment, of Paris, but the setting was more romantic than anything she had seen in Paris.

She descended into the shadowy street and the great doors swung open, revealing a wide stone archway. It was the sort of archway that cuts through the gatehouse of a mediaeval castle, and like so many of the archways she had already glimpsed, it opened into a courtyard. But she was sure there were not many courtyards like this one, not even in Valletta. She could see a sparkling fountain and a tree laden with oranges, a graceful stone statue and a mass of scarlet flowers. Iron lanterns swung from the roof of the archway and on the right-hand side, in a niche, a lamp burned before a tiny figure of the Virgin.

Catriona moved gratefully into the shadow of the doorway. A white-coated manservant appeared and began taking suitcases from Mario. Then Toni whirled past and subsided dramatically on to a wide stone seat. Resting her head against the wall behind her, she closed her eyes.

'Santa Maria! Peter, it's too hot, you can't make me stay here.'

Her brother studied her without emotion. 'You are going to live here,' he said firmly. 'Now go to your room. Carmen will look after you.'

An olive-skinned girl in crisp maid's uniform

appeared in one of the doorways opening off the passage, and with the limp grace of a ballet-dancer Toni got to her feet. Her lovely mouth was set in a sulky line, and she refused to look at her brother, but without another word she followed the maid out of sight.

Uncertain what to do, and feeling vaguely uncomfortable, Catriona stood looking around her. The Count touched her arm.

'In a moment,' he told her, 'Carmen will be back to take charge of you. While you are waiting, however, I would like to talk to you.'

He held open a door on the other side of the passage, and half blinded by the brilliance of the sunlight she moved through into a small, square room. The floor was of black marble, and she noticed that the heavy furnishings looked as if they had come mainly from seventeenth-century Spain. Two tall windows looked out through a grille on to the quiet street. An ebony crucifix hung on the wall beside the door.

The Count waved his hand in the direction of a chair. 'If you wish you may sit down, but I shall not detain you long.'

Catriona remained standing, her body tense. She was very aware of his dark eyes fixed on her. She had the absurd feeling that his intense dark gaze had the power to penetrate her soul.

'Antoinette is a spoilt child,' he said abruptly. 'She must be controlled. I should tell you that I expect you to do that.'

Catriona raised her eyebrows. 'I understood that I was to be your sister's companion, not her governess.'

'My sister is too old for a governess, but she is not too old for sensible supervision. You are, I understand, several years her senior and you appear to have an unusually strong will.' He moved over to a large desk that occupied one corner of the room. 'Use your will to control my sister, Miss Browne. That is all I ask.'

Catriona stared at him. 'But . . . she's just high-spirited. Just a schoolgirl!'

'She's silly and vulnerable, and liable to cause trouble, both for herself and for other people. I am placing you in charge of her. If you fail to do your job adequately it will, of course, be necessary to replace you.'

Catriona felt stupefied. She wanted to point out that in England, before they left, his definition of the job she would be doing had been altogether different. But no words would come.

An electric bell had been let into the wall beneath one of the windows, and when he pressed it Carmen appeared. She must, Catriona thought, have been waiting outside the door. The Count spoke to her in English.

'Carmen, when I telephoned this morning I gave instructions that a room was to be prepared for Miss Browne. I hope everything is ready?'

The maid smiled, revealing perfect white teeth. 'Yes, *signur*.'

'Good . . . *grazzi*.' He glanced at Catriona. 'I suggest that you go now, and rest. I shall hope to see you this evening.'

Catriona found that her room was situated at the far end of the house, overlooking a narrow side street. Its walls were starkly white, almost monastic in their bareness, but the furnishings were ornate and once again she was reminded of Spain. When Carmen left her alone she went straight to one of the windows and began struggling to open the tightly closed shutters. It was still only a quarter to five, but despite the presence of an electric fan the air was so oppressive that beads of perspiration were beginning to form on her forehead. After a few seconds she succeeded in pushing the shutters back, but immediately a wave of heat engulfed her, and she realised why it was that the maid had not attempted to open them. It was as if she had unfastened the door of an oven. Quickly she closed them again and in the warm dimness found herself wondering just exactly what kind of life she had let herself in for.

She was to be 'in charge' of Antoinette Caruana, but what exactly did that mean? In England the Count had told her that his sister needed nothing more than a companion. She would not have taken the job on any other terms, and she certainly had no intention of allowing herself to be turned into a watchdog. She would do the job she had originally been asked to do, but that was absolutely all.

Anyway, if Peter Vilhena wanted his eighteen-year-old sister to stay out of mischief, why had he brought her to live in the heart of the Maltese capital? Most people knew that Valletta was a bustling, cosmopolitan city. Its social life, Catriona would have thought, was likely to be fairly exotic. In such stimulating surroundings it might be extremely difficult to keep Toni Caruana's adventurous spirit firmly within the bounds imposed by her censorious half-brother. Besides, despite its obvious charm, Valletta clearly wasn't the best place to be during the last torrid days of August.

Slipping out of her skirt and blouse, Catriona lay

down on the embroidered counterpane that covered
the big sixteenth-century bed. So much had happened in just a few hours that she still found it difficult to take everything in, and when she closed her
eyes she had the strange feeling that the world was
revolving round her. Moist afternoon heat prickled
on her skin, but she was too deadly tired to let it
worry her any more. Valletta was very quiet. The
siesta hour had begun, and no sound came to her
through the louvred shutters, or through the oak
door leading to the corridor.

Within minutes she had dropped into a dreamless,
exhausted sleep.

CHAPTER FOUR

WHEN Catriona awoke, several hours later, she lay for a moment or two with her eyes closed. Then she became aware of a light, flickering draught. It was playing on her cheek, lifting the ends of her hair, and it felt pleasantly cool. Opening her eyes, she lay staring around her, and at first she found it difficult to remember where she was. She was in a very large bed, and the room was very large too, with a high ceiling. It made her feel small. There was nothing even slightly familiar about the place, and because the windows had been covered up she couldn't even see very much. . . .

Then everything came back. She sat up. Turning her head, she looked for the source of the draught, and immediately discovered that the electric fan was still humming quietly beside her. She pushed it away and lay back against a pile of pillows, trying to collect her thoughts.

The air was much less stuffy, and her ears detected a vague, distant murmur of sound. It was a sort of muffled hum composed of traffic noises, barking dogs and faint, indefinable rumbling sounds. It meant, obviously, that the siesta hour was over. Valletta was waking up.

Catriona glanced at her watch and made the discovery that it was a quarter to seven. What was it Carmen had said? When the Count was at home he usually dined at eight o'clock. She slid off the bed, found some slippers, and went over to one of the windows, pushing the shutters back. Outside, the air was much cooler and the sun had disappeared, leaving the sky a deep glowing turquoise. Already stars were glimmering above the flat rooftops, and evening was closing in on the city.

Catriona hung out, gazing across the narrow street at a building on the other side. Nearly opposite her window, there was a balcony hung with geraniums. As she watched, an elderly woman appeared on the balcony with a watering-can. A small, shrunken figure in rusty black, she watered the flowers thoroughly, then vanished again into the house, emerging a few seconds later with a large birdcage. The cage contained two brightly coloured budgerigars, and as the old woman placed it on a table she seemed to be talking to the birds. After a time she let them out, and one by one they fluttered to the balcony rail, but neither ventured beyond it. They belonged to the old woman's secret, flower-filled world, and they were held within it as if by a spell. Once again, Catriona was reminded of a half-forgotten fairy-tale, and she wondered if the whole island were enchanted.

Leaning farther out, she turned her head to the right and saw that the narrow side street sloped steeply downwards. At the far end, she glimpsed the slender *campanile* of a church, and beyond the *campanile* a pencil-like shaft of blue betrayed the nearness of the sea. It didn't look as if it could be more than half a mile away, and she remembered what Toni had said: Valletta was built on a peninsula.

More than anything she wanted to explore, to slip into a pair of old jeans and go for a walk, but that wasn't possible. When she looked at her watch she saw that it was now well past seven o'clock. She had to freshen up and change for dinner, and before doing that she needed to unpack.

Catriona's scanty wardrobe had not been improved by incarceration in a tightly packed suitcase. As she began putting things away in the vast hanging cupboard provided for the purpose, she realised, with a shock, that she had hardly anything suitable to wear. In England clothes had not presented any particular problem, and since she had recently purchased one or two summery items, she had imagined, when she packed that morning, that she was fairly well equipped for Malta. Now, for the very first time in her life, she felt almost ashamed of her own skimpy belongings. She only had a couple of crumpled cotton dresses, three pairs of jeans and a small selection of severely practical shirts and tops. None of it seemed exactly suitable for life in an aristocratic Maltese household. She didn't buy expensive clothes —she had never been able to afford them—and she didn't even own a pair of evening shoes. At least half her luggage was composed of painting equipment and as she looked at it, piled up in a corner of the room, she felt, just for a moment, faintly desperate.

Then she took a firm grip of herself. She was a struggling artist, not a member of the jet set. At the moment, she didn't spend money on clothes because she had priorities that were more important, and that wasn't going to change. Not just because she had entered the employment of Peter Vilhena, anyway. In the morning she might go out and buy another dress—perhaps a skirt too, and a top to go with it. But that would be her limit. She wasn't trying to compete with Antoinette.

Inspecting the blue, sleeveless dress that was her only possible choice for evening, she told herself firmly that there was nothing wrong with it. It was rather plain, but it had cost quite a lot more than anything else she possessed and it suited her. It had suffered badly in transit, and she wished that she had an iron, or at least that she had the courage to ring the bell and ask for one. The bell was beside her bed, and for a moment she almost pressed it, but then her nerve failed her. In her own way the maid was as well turned out as Toni. What on earth would she be likely to think of a girl who arrived from England with practically nothing to wear?

In the end, she resorted to the simple expedient of hanging the dress beside a window, and by the time she had taken a shower in the tiny bathroom adjoining her room it was beginning to recover fairly well. She brushed her hair and applied a little make-up, at the same time studying her reflection critically. In England the summer had been wet, and she hadn't acquired any tan at all, but now she noticed that on the way from the airport her nose had come into contact with too much sunshine and the fair, sensitive skin had reacted angrily. It was red and sore, but there was almost nothing she could do about it. Desperately she wondered if there might be some way she could camouflage the damage. It looked so dreadful. Then she suddenly caught herself up.

Did a thing like that really matter? Why was she getting so nervous about her appearance? Who was she trying to impress? Certainly not Count Vilhena. She told herself that she couldn't care less what he thought of her.

Cautiously she dabbed her nose with foundation cream, and the burnt area became a little less noticeable. After all, it was the sort of thing that could happen to anybody. By the time she was ready to go downstairs the blue dress had lost most of its creases and she decided that, on the whole, she didn't look too bad. In any case, it was doubtful whether anyone would even notice her.

Quietly she opened her bedroom door and stepped out into a gallery that seemed to run the entire length of the house. On the way up, attended by Carmen, she hadn't noticed very much, but now she saw that the walls were adorned with pikes and cutlasses, halberds and rapiers. They were souvenirs, presumably, of Malta's colourful history. Feeling that she ought to walk on tiptoe, she slipped along the gallery to the head of the uncarpeted marble staircase, her sandals making no sound as she crept downstairs.

In the long hall at the bottom she lingered again, gazing around her in awe. Though there was little furniture in sight, the walls were lined with portraits —a long succession of black-eyed men and women. There were Renaissance nobles in doublets of crimson, priests with thin, ascetic faces, veiled women whose white fingers were heavy with rings. All of them, she supposed, were members of the Vilhena family, wealthy, proud Maltese aristocrats.

They made her shiver and she turned away from them quickly. At one end of the hall a door opened into the passageway through which she had entered the house, and she hurried through it. She could hear the sound of voices. There seemed to be several of them and she guessed that they came from the courtyard. Though not usually shy, or particularly nervous, she felt a sudden urge to take flight.

But she knew she couldn't do that. Whoever these people were, she had to join them. Drawing a deep breath, she walked through the passage into the courtyard.

Between the fountain and some hibiscus bushes a table and chairs had been set out and in the scented coolness she saw a small group of people were enjoying aperitifs. Peter Vilhena was standing beside the fountain, his right hand caressing the head of a magnificent borzoi, and it occurred to her that he looked rather sombre. He didn't seem to be taking much part in the conversation.

Toni, wearing a glamorous sarong-style evening dress, was curled up on a pile of cushions in the shadow of the orange-tree. Her hair was hanging loose, cascading down her back, and heavy gold bangles weighted her wrists. She looked like a figure from the Arabian Nights.

But it wasn't Toni, or even her brother, who drew and held Catriona's attention. It was the third member of the group, a strikingly beautiful woman who was clad dramatically in scarlet.

Feeling more uncertain than she had ever felt in her entire adult life, Catriona stood hovering in the shadow of the archway. By comparison with the two women reclining in graceful attitudes in front of her she was going to look little more than ridiculous, and for the second time she began to consider seriously the possibility of retreat. Then Toni caught sight of her.

'Catriona . . . come and join us!'

All three heads turned in her direction, and Peter Vilhena accorded her an almost imperceptible bow.

She felt herself flushing, but with a determined effort she went forward to join them.

'Have a drink, Miss Browne.' There was no expression whatsoever on the Count's face, but she felt certain, nevertheless, that he was taking in every detail of her appearance.

Toni sent a friendly smile in her direction. 'Have a lemonade, if you don't want anything stronger,' she suggested. With an expressive gesture, she indicated the other woman present. 'This is Jacqueline Calleja. She is a friend of my brother's. I have been telling her about you.'

The scarlet beauty nodded graciously. She had perfect classical features, and the most beautiful brown eyes Catriona had ever seen, more striking even than Toni's. Her thick black hair had been twisted into gleaming plaits that coiled themselves around her head, and her mouth, like her dress, was flame-coloured.

'Hello,' said Catriona. She was beginning to wish that the ground would open and devour her, complete with the blue dress.

The vivid lips parted, smiling. 'But what a pity. Your luggage has not arrived, Miss Browne?'

Catriona felt as if the sunburn on her nose were spreading all over her body. 'I . . . my luggage is here,' she confessed awkwardly. 'I didn't bring much with me.'

'Ah!' Jacqueline Calleja smiled again. She gave the impression that she understood perfectly.

Toni intervened. 'The climate is so different here, and she hasn't had time to buy anything yet—we whisked her away at a moment's notice. It was too bad, but I'll take her shopping in the morning.' She collected some more cushions, and made them into a second pile. 'Come and sit here, Catriona.'

Still on fire with humiliation, Catriona sank gratefully on to the cushions. Then she saw that the Count was bending over her, holding out a glass.

'Iced lime-juice, with lemonade,' he said quietly. 'You will find it quite innocuous. Of course, if you would prefer something stronger. . . .'

She shook her head hastily. 'No. Thank you, that looks lovely.' As she took the drink from him, she noticed the strength in his lean brown fingers, and when they brushed lightly against her own she felt as if his controlled energy sent a shock through her body. At the same time, in some strange way the contact seemed to calm her, and involuntarily she glanced up at him. But he had already moved away and was leaning against the fountain, paying no attention to her. The Borzoi had lain down at his feet.

'Jacqueline is having dinner with us,' Toni said brightly. 'She is a television actress, and she's going to tell us about her work.'

'Not only television, darling.' Jacqueline sounded slightly piqued. 'I do take other parts as well, and my ambition is to be a very serious actress. I shall soon be playing in *Twelfth Night* . . . I'm to be Olivia. I know an English director who says that part could have been written for me.'

The Count set his glass down beside the fountain. 'On stage,' he remarked dryly, 'one beautiful woman is very much like another. It is in real life that her theatrical ability is put to the test.'

'Peter!' The husky, heavily accented voice was reproving and indulgent at the same time. 'You should not say things like that. Do you mean that we are always acting for your benefit?'

He looked down at the top of her gleaming head. 'Nearly always,' he said lightly. 'Some women, of course, are more talented than others, and consequently their performance is better—more convincing.'

Somewhere in the depths of the old stone house a gong began to boom. Toni jumped up at once. 'Let's go in, I'm so hungry.'

They dined in a quiet, white-walled room overlooking the street. As dusk began to fall, softly shaded lamps were lit and candles were placed on the table in front of them, but despite the approach of night it was still oppressively warm inside the house, and several electric fans whirred monotonously. Far off in the city a convent bell was tolling and Catriona began to feel that nothing was quite real. Could it be true that she had started the day in Berkshire—that only twenty-four hours ago she had been waiting at table in the dining-room of the Calverley Hotel? It was the sort of thing that only happened in novels. It was all too much to take in.

They ate stuffed aubergines, followed by salmon cooked in white wine, and Jacqueline obligingly kept her promise to tell them all about her work. She seemed to lead a busy life, and to be very much in demand. Watching her lovely, exotic face, following her graceful gestures, listening to her seductive voice, Catriona decided that there was one role she would fill to perfection—and that was the role of Countess Vilhena. It was a part, too, that she obviously wanted. As she sat at Peter's right hand, her back to a shadowy portrait, her eyes sparkling in the candleglow, she looked so staggeringly perfect that it was hardly surprising her host seemed to find difficulty in dragging his eyes away from her.

Catriona thought that surely it could not be long before he made up his mind. He had, it seemed, extensive business interests, mainly connected with boat-building, and he didn't appear to allow himself much free time, but he probably wouldn't find it difficult to make room in his life for Jacqueline. They would suit one another very well. She found them both almost equally infuriating.

As for the crazy idea that she had been steadied by the touch of his fingers—well, that was something she had imagined. She was probably more tired than she realised.

At last they reached the coffee stage, and Jacqueline drew her chair back. She looked at Peter beneath her lashes.

'Darling, it's very sad, but I must go.'

He leant back in his chair, tapping lightly on the table. 'Why?' he asked.

'Because there is a party I must not miss.' She shrugged, and stood up. 'I would not bother about it, but it is a family celebration—my sister's wedding anniversary. You know, she has been married for twelve years.'

The Count's brow puckered. 'No, I did not know. You must forgive me, Jacqueline. I had forgotten that you had a sister old enough to have reached such a milestone.'

She looked down at him. With one beautifully manicured finger she touched his hand as it lay on the table. 'I didn't say anything earlier because I thought it would spoil dinner. I know you wouldn't want to go with me, darling.'

'No.' He looked at the slender finger still caressing the fine dark hairs on the back of his hand. 'No.' he repeated abruptly. 'You were right.'

'Ah, well, never mind.' She smiled brightly. Then her glance fell on Toni, and an idea seemed to strike her. 'Antoinette, you're not doing anything? Not tonight?'

Toni looked at her eagerly. 'No. . . .'

'Well then, you must come with me.' She turned to the Count, her eyes full of appeal. 'Let her come. It will be a very respectable party.'

Peter Vilhena glanced at his sister. 'You may go if you wish. You will be safe with Jacqueline.'

Toni's eyes lit, and for a moment Catriona thought she was going to kiss her brother, but if any such idea did pass through her head she dismissed it. Instead, she said:

'Thank you. Thank you, Peter!'

To Catriona's relief the invitation obviously did not extend to her. She saw Toni looking at her anxiously, and knew that the other girl would have liked to press for her inclusion. But it would clearly have been difficult for Jacqueline Calleja to envisage the possibility of treating a paid employee as an equal.

When they had gone she lingered for a moment in the courtyard, under the far-off night sky. There were thousands of stars overhead, and she supposed the same stars were looking down on England, even if, at the moment, they might be hidden behind rain-clouds, and yet her own familiar world seemed light years away. It was as if she had crashed through a magic barrier into some other dimension, and her old life had been left behind. All at once she felt lonely and rather flat, and that shook her, because she was used to being alone.

On the way up to her bedroom she passed the door that led to Peter Vilhena's study. A light glowed beneath it, and she wondered what he was doing. She imagined him sitting at the big desk in the corner, his dark head bent, and she wondered whether he was thinking of Jacqueline.

Upstairs, she wrote a short letter to the elderly aunt who was her only surviving relative, and then she got into bed. Her windows were wide open now, to the starlit night, and when she closed her eyes it seemed to her that she could hear the soft breathing of the city. But she hadn't lost her feeling of isolation, and even in sleep she could not escape from it. She began to dream that she was alone in a small boat, drifting helplessly on unfamiliar seas, without even a compass to guide her. It was night, in her dream, and she seemed to see nothing but the faint glow of star-shine, reflected on the surface of still waters. There was no land in sight, and she knew that there wasn't going to be.

When she had been asleep for three or four hours, she awoke with a start to find that someone was tapping softly at her door. Lifting herself on one elbow, she switched on the bedside lamp, then reached for the towelling dressing-gown that she had left lying across the foot of the bed.

'Who's there?' she called sharply.

The door opened, and a head appeared. 'Catriona——? Are you awake?'

Catriona sat up in bed. According to her watch, it was ten past two. 'What's the matter?' she asked in bewilderment.

Toni closed the door soundlessly and danced across the room to perch on the end of the bed.

'I'm sorry, did I really wake you up? I just wanted to tell you what a wonderful party it was. It's a shame you didn't go.'

'I didn't feel much like going to a party,' Catriona told her honestly. 'Not tonight.' She yawned, and wondered whether the other girl made a habit of rousing people from sleep every time she felt the urge to talk. 'I'm glad you had fun, anyway. Were there many people there?'

'Not really.' Toni's eyes were very bright, and there was a peach-coloured flush in her cheeks. 'It was just a lovely party, that's all.' She sighed dreamily. 'Jacqueline's sister lives in the Old City. It's beautiful up there.'

'I thought this was the old city,' Catriona objected, feeling an unreasoning antipathy towards Jacqueline's sister.

'It isn't as old as Mdina. We'll be going up there one day soon, and then you'll understand. There's nothing quite like it anywhere else in the world.' Humming softly beneath her breath, she got up and drifted over to the dressing-table. Gazing into the mirror, she gathered her hair into a coil and wound it around her head. 'What do you think?' she asked. 'Does it make me look older?'

Abandoning all hope of getting back to sleep within the foreseeable future, Catriona thought the matter over. 'Why do you want to look older?' she asked.

'Oh—I don't know.' Toni's colour deepened a little. 'People take you more seriously, don't they? If you're not just a schoolgirl.'

'People take you seriously if you stick to being

yourself, if you behave like a real person. Whatever your age happens to be.'

'Well, maybe. . . . It depends who you are, really. I expect you were always taken seriously. You're so positive and strong-minded, not like most girls.'

'Am I?' Catriona smiled wryly.

'Of course you are. You're—I suppose you're what men call "interesting". You could have lots of exciting love affairs, if you wanted to.'

'Thank you, but I don't want lots of exciting love affairs. Now, don't you think it's time you went to bed?'

'Okay, I'll go.' Toni tiptoed to the door. 'But in the morning we'll go out, and you must do some shopping. If you haven't got very much money Peter will give you an advance on your salary.'

Catriona felt as if her skin were starting to crawl with embarrassment. 'We'll go shopping if you like, but I don't need an advance from your brother. Not just yet.' Firmly, she put out a hand to extinguish the light. 'Goodnight.'

Toni hesitated a second, sighed deeply, then flashed her a brilliant smile.

'See you in the morning.'

CHAPTER FIVE

CATRIONA awoke at half past eight to find Carmen entering her room with a breakfast tray. The air was already stifling, and through the open window she could see that the sky was a deep cobalt blue. She felt guilty.

'I should have been up ages ago,' she told Carmen. 'I'm not a guest. I have a job to do.'

The maid smiled. 'You want to be all alone? In Palazzo Vilhena, no one gets up for breakfast.'

Seated by the window, sipping coffee and nibbling a warm croissant, Catriona started thinking about Toni. The Maltese girl had obviously had fun the night before, and there didn't seem to be much doubt that she was going to find her native island pleasanter than she had anticipated. Perhaps Jacqueline Calleja would be assuming responsibility for her social well-being. After all, they might one day be sisters. If things did work out that way, though, Catriona knew she would soon be out of a job. There would simply be no reason for her to stay on.

Oh, well, at least she would have had a holiday. And she might even manage to get some useful work done.

Slipping into a slightly outdated sundress, she went downstairs, and in the long hall she joined forces with Toni. The other girl was looking glamorous in candy pink shorts, teamed with a skimpy white top, and Catriona felt slightly taken aback.

'Will you be all right like that?' she asked. 'I mean
—don't you have to be careful in Catholic countries?'

Toni laughed. 'Not in Malta, not now. They're
too used to tourists. Of course, I couldn't go into a
church like this, but this morning we're just going to
do some shopping. We must hurry, though. By half
past eleven it will be too hot to move.'

They set out to walk through the shadowy streets,
and Toni explained that in Valletta cars were used as
little as possible. At one time, it seemed, congestion
had been a serious problem, but eventually the
Government had devised an extra road tax, to be
paid on any vehicle that was to be driven inside the
capital, and the new restriction had been very effective in checking the flow of traffic. For those who felt
they needed transport there were regular mini-bus
services, but in most cases Catriona could see that it
was probably quite easy to walk. There were so
many short cuts, and where the gradient was particularly steep the pavement had often been replaced by
flights of steps.

Following Toni along ancient alleyways and
through graceful Renaissance arcades, Catriona was
enchanted by everything she saw. She soon discovered that Valletta was an intimate little city, an
elaborately planned enclave designed and built in
the sixteenth century at the instigation of one man,
Jean Parisot de la Valette, Grand Master of the
Order of St. John. For two and a half centuries,
Malta's history had been closely bound up with the
Knights of St. John, an order of celibate Crusaders
whose original mission had been the protection of
Jerusalem and the care of Christian pilgrims to the
Holy Land. In 1291 the Knights had been driven out

of Palestine, and for a time had taken refuge on the
Greek island of Rhodes, but eventually a consolidated
Turkish attack had driven them farther westwards,
and in 1530 they had established themselves on
Malta. Five years later the Turkish fleet had followed
them, but after a long and bitter siege Malta had
emerged victorious, becoming famous throughout
Christendom for her noble stand against the forces of
Islam. La Valette had decided to celebrate by building a fine new capital city, mainly, it seemed, for the
accommodation of his Knights, and Valletta had
been the result. In their new, purpose-built city the
Knights were magnificently catered for, and each
langue or national group was allotted its own splendid
house. Four of the lovely Renaissance *auberges* had
been destroyed during the Second World War, but
five, it seemed, were still standing, and most were in
use as public buildings. The Auberge d'Italie, which
they passed in the course of their walk, had become
the National Museum, and the Auberge de Castille
was now the official residence of the Maltese Prime
Minister.

'Being Maltese,' Toni said thoughtfully, 'my ancestors did not like the Knights.' As they passed, she
glanced up at the windows of the Auberge d'Italie.
'In a sense they were invaders, after all, and there
was much resentment. But they left us beautiful
buildings, and many other things of which we are
proud.' She laughed. 'Now we sell them to the
tourists.'

But Valletta was not entirely a place of ancient
memories. Republic Street, once known as Kings-
way, was the central thoroughfare, and it was lined
with up-to-the-minute shops. Prices, on the whole,

tended to be lower than in England, and the display
windows attracted hordes of foreign shoppers. Catriona bought two insubstantial sundresses, a bikini—
on Toni's advice—and some pretty Italian sandals.
Since she rarely allowed herself the fun of buying
clothes she was almost childishly pleased with her
purchases, and felt that she had gone quite far
enough, but Toni still wasn't satisfied. She pointed
out that the English girl possessed nothing in the way
of evening wear, and she clearly felt that something
should be done about such a situation.

Catriona couldn't see that in her position she was
going to have very much need for evening wear, but
in the end she allowed herself to be tempted by a
slender embroidered skirt, and to go with it she purchased a silk top. The top was pearly pink, like a
cowrie shell, and rather to her surprise it did things
for her soft English colouring. She had always been
fairly unadventurous where clothes were concerned,
mainly because she couldn't afford to be anything
else, but now she realised that she ought to experi-
ment more often.

Well satisfied with what she evidently felt to have
been a good morning's work, Toni suggested that
they should now treat themselves to a lunchtime
snack, and she led the way to a big Italian-style café
situated opposite the Royal Malta Library. The café
was obviously popular as a rendezvous, both with
Maltese and with foreigners, and it was crowded.
When they sat down, Toni attracted a good deal of
attention, and Catriona noticed that she seemed
happily conscious of the fact. Over the top of a
brimming milk-shake, she smiled mischievously at
the other girl.

'I like being looked at,' Toni remarked with naïve candour. 'Do you think that's a terrible thing to say? Perhaps I should mention it the next time I go to Confession.'

'Perhaps you should be an actress,' Catriona suggested. 'You could ask Miss Calleja for her advice.'

Toni wrinkled her nose. 'I don't like Jacqueline.'

'I thought you had a wonderful time last night.'

'That had nothing to do with her.' Toni put her milk-shake down and sighed. Obviously, she was recalling once again the delights of the previous evening. Catriona strongly suspected that there had been someone very special at the party she had attended, and she wondered whether Toni planned to see him again. But she doubted whether it would be a good idea to ask, so she stuck to the subject of Jacqueline.

'Miss Calleja seems to get on well with your brother,' she said rather dryly.

'She wants him,' Toni remarked, making substantial inroads on a large doughy cheesecake. 'If she's clever, she may even get him, too. Peter likes them hard and beautiful—like Venetian glass.'

'Glass can break,' Catriona pointed out. 'Miss Calleja doesn't look particularly fragile.'

'No, that's true.' Toni demolished the last of the cheesecake. 'She's more like very strong plastic—you know, poly-something. She must be dreadful to work with. Still,' smiling slightly, 'I should be grateful to her. After last night, Valletta doesn't seem so bad.'

'It's still very hot,' Catriona pointed out.

'Yes, but that doesn't really worry me.' She looked a little selfconscious. 'I was disappointed when Peter said we were coming here, but that was mainly because I thought Gozo would be more fun. It's another island, you know, off the north coast. Everyone goes there in August, and Peter has boatyards over there. He has a nice modern villa, too. It was only built about five years ago. There's an old family house, somewhere, but that's just a ruin now.' Leaning back in her chair, she stretched like a cat, and masculine heads turned. We must all go to Gozo one day. You would love it.'

'M'mm, that would be nice,' Catriona agreed. 'If your brother doesn't mind.'

'I don't care if he does,' Toni retorted. 'He doesn't own either of us.' She stood up. 'Come on, let's do something interesting.'

They spent the next hour or so having their hair done in an air-conditioned, ultra-modern salon below the level of the street. Against a background of murals depicting sunlit Mediterranean beaches, five or six stylists worked with feverish efficiency, colouring, conditioning and shaping. They were obviously expert at their craft, and when they had finished with Catriona she barely recognised herself. They had cut her hair very short, carefully moulding it to suit the contours of her face, and in the process she had been endowed with an intriguing elfin charm. Her grey eyes looked huge and wistful, as they stared back at her from the mirror, and her mouth curved beguilingly.

When they climbed back into the daylight, Toni nodded approvingly. 'That's really something. Don't you feel different?'

'Yes,' she confessed. 'It's a bit unnerving. I'm used to being me.'

'Don't you want to be glamorous?'

'I'm here to do a job,' Catriona reminded her.

'Yes, but wouldn't you like to have all sorts of gorgeous men running after you?'

'They're not likely to run after me, and I'm not even sure I want them to.'

Back at Palazzo Vilhena, Toni announced her intention of taking a siesta, but before they separated at the head of the stairs she had a sudden idea.

'I thought——' she hesitated. 'Tomorrow, maybe, we'll go round the island. There's such a lot that you have to see, and Mario can drive us. But I thought that if you wanted to paint, there's a wonderful view from the Barracca Gardens. We could go there this afternoon. Later on, when it's cool and we have rested. The Gardens are high above Grand Harbour.'

'I'd like that.' Feeling as if she might be on the edge of collapse from heat exhaustion, Catriona forced herself to smile enthusiastically. 'I really would—later on.' Provided, she thought, that she survived the afternoon.

Upstairs, in the peace of her own room, she dropped limply on to the bed and almost immediately fell into a deep sleep.

Two hours later, however, she awoke feeling much better, and when they set out for the Barracca Gardens she took some of her painting equipment, just in case. Normally she tended to shy away from the things she was told she would want to paint—their charm was usually a good deal too unsubtle—but this was the Mediterranean, and if the view really did turn out to be spectacular she might want to do something about it.

The Barracca Gardens occupied a part of the town's old ramparts, and they had been there for a very long time, an oasis of green in a desert of yellow stone. Within the gardens there were shady walks and quiet, secluded arbours, spreading pepper trees and walls hung with the trailing fire of crimson bougainvillaea. When Catriona came to the narrow platform overlooking the harbour she was more than enchanted.

Malta's Grand Harbour, she knew, was one of the world's outstanding natural havens, and from earliest times Mediterranean man had exploited its possibilities to the utmost. She had known that since she was in the Fourth Form at school. But nothing she had read could ever have prepared her for the view that met her eyes when she leant over an iron parapet and gazed down on the famous harbour itself. It was an enormous inlet, divided, as far as she could see, into at least three bays, and it was surrounded by ancient honey-coloured fortifications. There seemed to be a number of docks, all of them busy, and the vast expanse of water was dotted with shipping of every size and description. A little white liner was just coming in, passing between twin forts that looked towards the open sea, and a line of tankers lay at anchor below the gardens. But though the life of the port was absorbing, Catriona's attention was held by the splendour of the colours spread out in front of her, the azure sea, the golden walls bathed in evening light.

She felt an immediate urge to capture it all on canvas, to hold it in such a way that it could never be lost. Smiling, she turned to Toni, who was watching her expectantly.

'It's fantastic,' she said. 'Do you think we could stay here for an hour? You were absolutely right, I must do something about this.'

Toni was gratified. 'Of course, that's why I brought you here.' She looked at her watch. 'You have plenty of time. It's only six o'clock.'

Hardly able to take her eyes off the view, Catriona unfolded her easel. 'Yes, but what will you do with yourself? You can't just stand and watch me.'

· 'The shops are open now, and I want to buy a new bikini. I forgot, when we were shopping this morning, and there's a place just two minutes from here. I won't be long.' Before turning away, she hesitated. 'You don't mind being alone, do you?'

'Of course not.' Already seated on the folding stool which was a vital part of her painting equipment, Catriona began squeezing colours on to the worn palette she had acquired when she was still at school. 'Run along and pick your bikini. Don't get anything too daring, though. Your brother might not approve.'

Toni laughed. 'I won't!'

When she was gone, Catriona started work. She might not be able to do much, not tonight, but there would be other evenings. First of all she sketched out a rough impression of the scene in front of her, then she started to apply colour. She wanted to capture the light—the luminous glow that meant the sun was beginning to sink towards the west—and she worked as quickly as she could, her brush moving deftly over the canvas. The gardens lay in shadow now, behind their curtain of trees, and the air was pleasantly cool. A few people wandered past, and occasionally a couple stopped to glance over her shoulder before moving on again, but no one disturbed her. She realised that, as a people, the Maltese were both too sensitive and too reserved to obtrude upon anyone's privacy.

She had been working for some time, and was making good progress when a shadow fell across her painting. She looked up, expecting to see another curious stroller—and gaspèd. The Count was standing beside her, and he seemed very tall. He seemed very threatening, too. She started, putting a hand to her face, and a streak of chrome yellow appeared on her nose.

Somehow she blurted out, 'I didn't know you were there.'

'I am quite sure you did not.' His voice was dangerously calm. 'You have been here long?' he asked.

'I. . . .' She glanced at her watch, and realised with a guilty shock that, while she was working, an hour had passed. 'It's later than I thought,' she said, a little annoyed with herself. 'Toni suggested I might like to paint this view, and she had some shopping to do. I'm waiting for her to come back.'

'And when are you expecting her?'

'She should have been here by now,' Catriona admitted. She felt rather conscience-stricken because it hadn't occurred to her before that Toni had been a long time. Though, after all, the girl wasn't a baby. There really was no earthly reason why she shouldn't take her time over a visit to the shops. For that matter, there was no reason why she should need round-the-clock supervision.

'Antoinette will not be rejoining you.' The Count's voice was like steel.

'Not . . .' Catriona stared up at him, her eyes wide. 'Have—have you seen her?'

'Yes, I've seen her. And I've sent her home.' His cycs glinted down at her. 'I was leaving the office of my lawyer, in Merchant Street, when I happened to pass a certain café. I glanced through the window, and was surprised to see my sister drinking coffee at a corner table. She was sharing the table with a young man,'

Catriona digested this. It looked as if Toni had met a friend. Well, what was wrong with that?

'She must have run into someone . . . I suppose.'

'My sister does not wander the streets of Valletta, alone, "running into" young men.'

For a moment Catriona was almost too astonished to speak. 'Who was the man?' she asked at last. 'Did you know him?'

'He is a notorious playboy. I would not normally allow him to come within a mile of my sister.' He paused, and she realised that he was breathing deeply. 'I have spoken with him, and I hope he understands the situation. I have made it clear that if he approaches Antoinette again the consequences will be extremely serious—for himself.'

Carefully, Catriona replaced her palette in its worn case. Then she stood up. 'You can't do that sort of thing,' she said.

'I can, and I will.' There was a tremor of pure fury in his voice. Suddenly his fingers gripped Catriona's wrist, so tightly that she almost cried out in pain. 'My sister, Miss Browne, is not an English girl. Until she marries—and especially while she is in my house— she will conduct herself like a Maltese girl of good character.' His hold tightened. 'You will *not* allow her to wander the streets alone!'

Catriona was so angry that she felt all the colour leave her face. 'Your sister,' she pointed out, 'is a fully grown woman. When I left England I did not understand that I would be expected to spy on her. Why shouldn't she have coffee with a friend? How could a meeting like that be anything but completely innocent? If you want her to behave well you'll have to trust her. You can't degrade me by depriving her of all freedom. You can't degrade me by asking me to be your watchdog.' Swallowing, she looked down at his fingers, still holding her wrist in a remorseless grip. 'I'll fly home tomorrow. I'm sorry you've been put to the inconvenience of importing such an unsatisfactory employee. When I get back to England I'll send you the money for my fare.'

He released her wrist, and she saw him staring at the livid marks left by the pressure of his fingers. 'You must do as you wish,' he said quietly.

'I certainly will.' Trembling with anger, Catriona struggled to fold her easel up, but its ungainly legs jammed. For a moment or two the Count simply stared, then muttering under his breath he came to her rescue, folding it up without difficulty. He placed it under one arm, and then gathered up the remainder of her belongings.

'My car is outside the gates,' he told her.

Inside the low-slung Citroën, Catriona stared resolutely through the windscreen. She felt furious with the man beside her, and with everything he stood for. He had no right to make his young sister's life a misery, and he had no right, either, having dragged her out from England, to treat her like an unsatisfactory servant. She had been beginning to like Malta very much—she knew it was a place she could come to love, but he had ruined everything. She couldn't go on working for a man who behaved as he did. It wasn't possible.

The car swung in a wide circle, then plunged back into a maze of Valletta streets. Catriona felt as if something were aching, deep inside her, and she could almost have cried. It had been so beautiful in the gardens, so peaceful, and she had been pleased, too, with the work she had accomplished. Now it would have to be scrapped.

In front of Palazzo Vilhena he moved round to open the car door for her, but before he had an opportunity to touch it she sprang out unaided. Her easel, the case containing her colours and her folding stool were all in the back of the car and he remarked that he would have them sent up to her.

'Thank you,' she said, 'but I'll take them myself.'

He shrugged. 'Very well.'

With a certain amount of difficulty Catriona carried her equipment into the house. Not glancing at her again, the Count got back into his car and drove it away to its garage.

CHAPTER SIX

WHEN she reached the door of her own room Catriona had a certain amount of difficulty in turning the handle, but as soon as she was inside she dropped all her burdens and leaned against the closed door. For a moment she shut her eyes, while helpless resentment swept over her. Then a sound caught her attention, and she opened her eyes abruptly.

Toni was lying face down on the bed, sobbing violently. Catriona thought for a moment, then went over and shook the other girl lightly by the shoulder.

'Hello! It's me, Catriona.'

The sobs subsided and slowly Toni rolled over on to her back. Her eyes were red and swollen, her face streaked with tears.

'Did he bring you back?' she asked huskily.

'Yes.' Catriona sat down on the bed. She examined her own paint-stained fingers. 'I'm sorry, Toni, but I don't think I can take any more of your brother. I'm going back to England.'

'No, you can't!' Toni sat up, her face even more a mask of distress than it had been a few seconds earlier. 'Please, it will be dreadful if you go. There is no one else, except. . . .' She stopped, and her colour deepened.

'Except the boy you met this afternoon?'

'My . . . my brother told you about Vittorio?'

Catriona nodded. 'He told me that he found you having coffee with a friend.'

'He's the boy I told you about . . . do you remember? When we were talking, on the plane?'

'I remember.'

'His name is Vittorio Falzon. I . . . I liked him a lot, even when I first met him. You must have guessed.'

The older girl smiled a little. 'You obviously found him attractive.'

'Yes, but it was more than that. Then, last night, at the party, I met him again. He remembered me—really remembered, I mean. He said he had been wondering when I was coming back to Malta. We talked and danced, and—I suppose nothing else seemed to matter. Then he asked when I would be able to meet him somewhere, and I didn't know what to say. I knew that if I went out alone Peter would want to know why, and it all seemed so difficult. But I thought that if you and I went out together, and I arranged things so that I could go off by myself for a while. . . .' Toni broke off. 'I'm sorry. It wasn't fair, but I thought nobody would find out.'

Catriona stood up. 'Nobody would have found out if your brother hadn't caught sight of you, and there's no need to apologise to me. Why shouldn't you meet a friend for coffee? You're quite old enough. . . .' She shrugged. 'Oh, it's all absurd. Anyway, I've told your brother what I think of him.'

'You . . . what did you say?' Toni's eyes widened.

'I've told Count Vilhena that he can't go on behaving like this. It won't make any difference, I'm afraid, but at least I said it. And I really will have to go.'

'No! No, I can't do without—without someone to talk to.'

'You'll make friends,' Catriona pointed out. 'Presumably your brother won't object to girl friends.'

'They wouldn't be like you. They wouldn't know what to do.'

'I don't know what to do,' Catriona said honestly. 'If you want my advice, though. . . .' She hesitated, and Toni looked at her expectantly. 'Couldn't you get in touch with your father? I'm sure he'd agree that—that Count Vilhena is being very unreasonable. A letter from him might make all the difference.'

Toni shook her head emphatically. 'My father is a very long way away, and he trusts Peter absolutely. If Peter is being hard on me, Father will think that perhaps he has reason. Anyway, he won't interfere.'

'Well then, I'd tell them both that you must have a job. Or you could try getting into university.'

Toni sighed, and shook her head again. 'I'm not clever enough for university, and Peter would never, never, never allow me to have a job.'

'In that case . . .' Catriona was beginning to feel impatient, 'grin and bear it, until you find a boy you want to marry.'

Toni's mouth drooped broodingly. And at that moment someone tapped lightly on the door. Catriona jumped.

'Come in!'

The door opened and Carmen appeared. 'If you have time, Miss Browne, *is-Signur* is waiting to speak with you.'

Looking at the maid anxiously, Toni said something in Maltese. As she replied, Carmen smiled nervously.

'I asked if he is in a bad temper,' Toni explained

for the benefit of the English girl. 'She says she doesn't know.'

'It doesn't matter,' Catriona said quietly. She glanced at Carmen. 'If Count Vilhena wants to see me I'll come down.'

Toni fixed her with an imploring look. 'Please tell him you're going to stay.'

Peter Vilhena was seated at the desk in his own private sanctum, the room she had seen when she first arrived. Letters and papers lay scattered in front of him, and he had evidently been attempting to concentrate on them, but as soon as the door closed behind Catriona he pushed them aside and got to his feet.

'Sit down, please.'

She obeyed, watching him warily.

'I hope you have reconsidered your decision to leave us.' He was standing with his back to one of the windows, as graceful and elegant as a panther, but his head was bent and she couldn't read the expression on his face.

'I. . . . Actually, no, I haven't. I've been talking to Antoinette.'

'Ah! She was waiting for you?'

'She was very distressed.'

'I am sure that she was.' He shot her a keen glance. 'You feel perhaps that I do not treat her kindly enough. If I would only allow her complete freedom —well then, no doubt she would not be distressed. Eventually, of course, she would begin to suffer the consequences of complete freedom, but that she does not understand. I think you do not understand it either.'

Catriona stared at him in bewilderment. 'She has

to grow up some time. You can't supervise her for ever.'

'Until Antoinette acquires a husband I shall continue to hold myself responsible for her well-being. I shall certainly do everything in my power to ensure that she does not associate with undesirable young men.'

'Someone has to help her grow up, though. Eventually she'll need to make her own decisions.'

He turned his head to look out of the window, and Catriona once again became aware how good-looking he was. His strongly moulded features were classically even, his eyelashes long and thick. If only he were a different sort of man he would be extremely attractive.

'Children are taught to avoid fire,' he said suddenly, 'to treat it with respect. If they are not given such necessary instruction they may burn themselves, perhaps seriously. Of course, I am aware that in England young women frequently learn the lessons of life in precisely that kind of way—they are allowed to learn by experience, and sometimes are badly burned.' He looked at her gravely, his dark eyes intent. 'I have no wish to probe into your personal life, Miss Browne, but if you have so far escaped this sort of experience you are fortunate.'

Catriona shook her head. 'I can manage my own life,' she said quietly. 'So, I'm sure, could your sister, if she were allowed to.'

Almost absentmindedly, he glanced at his watch. 'It's nearly half past seven,' he remarked, as if this discovery surprised him a little. His glance rested once again on Catriona, and she realised that for the first time he was noticing the change in her appearance. Absurdly, she began to feel selfconscious, but he didn't comment. Instead, he looked rather wearily at the papers littering his desk and remarked that he had a good deal of work to do.

'There are various matters that must be attended to this evening. However, the problem of Antoinette is also of serious importance.' He hesitated, then came to a decision. 'I would like to show you something,' he said abruptly, 'but I am afraid it will be necessary for you to have dinner with me. How soon can you be ready?'

'You mean—go out to dinner with you?' Catriona was aware she must have sounded startled.

'You feel the experience might prove too painful?' he suggested dryly. 'Even if you are determined to leave us, however, I think you should allow me this one opportunity to prove my point.' He looked at her again, and this time his eyes held hers. She felt almost as if she were being hypnotised.

'I'd rather not . . .' she began.

'You would prefer not to be under any kind of obligation to me?' He smiled rather oddly. 'You need not worry about that, I am not promising you a pleasant evening.'

'It isn't necessary. I—I've decided I will stay on. If you want me to.'

His face betrayed no reaction whatsoever. After a tiny pause he said coolly: 'Excellent. I'm so glad you have decided to be sensible. I would still be grateful, however, if you would have dinner with me.'

'All right, if you think it's important. But I'll have to change.'

He shook his head. 'There is no need for that. In any case, if we delay much longer we may not get a table.' He stood up. 'I shall expect to see you in five minutes. My car will be outside the door.'

Catriona didn't want to co-operate. She wanted to oppose him in every possible way, but something seemed to have happened to her will. She knew he was going to subject her to some bizarre kind of experience, but somehow she couldn't say 'no'.

She went up to her room, and finding that Toni had vanished wondered briefly whether she ought to look for the other girl and tell her what was happening. In the end, having taken a hurried shower and run a comb through her hair, she simply left a message with Carmen, who had come in to turn down her bed. After all, she wouldn't be very long. Nothing the Maltese Islands had to offer could induce her to linger over dinner with Peter Vilhena.

When she went down again she found him waiting for her in the street. He was leaning against the bonnet of his car, staring broodingly at the pavement, his fine dark brows drawn together, and when Catriona appeared he stared at her blankly, as if he had difficulty in remembering who she was.

Without a word, he put her into the car, and she began to feel increasingly angry. Whatever he was seeking to prove, she disliked his method of setting about it, just as she disliked everything about him. In the end she had decided not to leave, but it was only because of Toni, who at the moment needed a friend even more than Catriona herself needed her freedom.

They drove out of Valletta, taking a road which led them through a series of well-ordered suburbs. The streets were lined with neat, brightly painted houses, and she noticed that the people looked cheerful and prosperous. Black-haired children played noisily on the pavements. Everywhere there were strolling couples, good-looking boys and pretty girls, their arms entwined about each other. Catriona glanced sideways at the Count.

'Some young people,' she remarked, 'seem to have a good deal of freedom, even in Malta.'

He was silent for a moment. 'Young men and women go out together, yes,' he acknowledged evenly. 'Before such a thing is allowed, however, the girl's parents will usually make extensive enquiries. The boy must be a person they can approve of. He must have a job, and he must be a good Catholic. That is very important.'

Catriona stared thoughtfully at a couple standing near the edge of the kerb. 'I can see that his religion would be important,' she conceded. 'But—no job, no girl-friend. That's hard, isn't it?'

'Life is hard,' he pointed out, frowning a little as he negotiated a particularly dangerous right-hand bend

They reached the town of Sliema, a busy resort three miles from Valletta, and Catriona looked around her with interest. Sliema had an imposing promenade, numberless hotels and a large selection of smart shops. It was alive and bustling, and there was a very modern feel about it. He told her that it was a Mecca for tourists from all over the world.

'Many Maltese feel that it is a place one is wise to avoid,' he remarked. 'At least between May and September.'

Night had fallen now, and the sky was ablaze with stars. Sliema faced the open sea, and it was possible, too, to look across an intervening harbour to the lights of Valletta. There seemed to be a lot of cafés

and brightly-lit bars, and the streets were thronged
with people who were apparently out to enjoy themselves. They passed through the graceful Victorian
streets of the old town, then turned into a side street
and stopped. There was a sound of rock music, and
Catriona glanced round, wondering where it was
coming from.

The Count opened her door for her, and in silence
he helped her out, his fingers cold and hard against
her warm skin. For a fraction of a second she looked
up into his face, and realised with a shock that it was
like a mask. He led her down a brightly lit passageway between two buildings, and as he pushed her in
front of him through a low doorway she felt as if she
were stepping into some kind of inferno.

They were in a small, overcrowded night-club and
peering through a stifling haze of cigarette smoke she
could see that there was barely room to move. The
noise, which was ear-splitting, emanated from a six-
piece rock group which had been squeezed into an
alcove facing the bar, and a dozen or so couples were
swaying languorously to the beat. Many-coloured,
constantly changing lights flickered over them and
over the shadowy faces of others who were seated at
the tables. There seemed to be hardly an air.

Catriona had been in night-spots before, but she
had never seen anything quite like this. The heat and
the lack of space combined to give it the quality of a
nightmare.

The place was crowded almost to capacity, but
there was still one table vacant, and without the
slightest loss of composure Peter Vilhena cleaved a
way towards it. It was difficult to move an inch without being jostled, but with the Count's firm fingers

lightly clasping her elbow Catriona found that the crowd tended to part in front of her. They reached the vacant table, and a perspiring boy with black curly hair arrived to place a tattered menu in front of them. Peter surveyed the untidy scrawl with distaste.

'The melon,' he requested, after a moment's consideration. 'And the *timpana*—for both of us.' He glanced at Catriona. 'You would like an aperitif?'

She shook her head. 'I don't drink.'

'Really?' His brows ascended sharply. 'A tomato juice, then, for the *signurina*.' He pushed the grubby menu away and leant back in his chair. In front of them a very young girl was dancing with a man who was obviously a good deal older than she was, and several people were staring at her. Her dress left very little to the imagination, and it was abundantly clear that she had had more than enough to drink. Without the support of her companion's arms she looked as if she might have fallen. As they watched, her escort half led, half carried her back to their table, where she subsided, giggling weakly, in an oddly pathetic heap.

Catriona looked at Peter Vilhena. 'That girl can't be more than sixteen.' In order to make him hear she had to raise her voice.

He shrugged. 'Young people must have their freedom,' he reminded her.

The melon arrived with reasonable speed, but Catriona barely touched hers. The hot, sticky atmosphere was beginning to make her feel sick. She was struggling against a mixture of nausea and resentment. She understood very well why Peter had brought her to such a place, but although she was

faintly revolted by the scene in front of her she failed
to see that it had any bearing on the argument over
Toni. As far as that went, he was wasting his time,
and when they got outside she would tell him so. At
the moment, serious conversation was out of the
question.

The *timpana* arrived, and she forced herself to taste
a mouthful or two. It turned out to be a sort of Maltese cottage pie, containing large quantities of rather
rubbery macaroni. Catriona managed a few forkfuls,
then abandoned the struggle. Her head was beginning to ache.

'Have another tomato juice,' the Count suggested, watching her thoughtfully over the rim of his
own glass.

'No, thank you.'

'Something stronger, then. Perhaps you're getting
the feel of the place.'

She didn't answer. Their table was situated only a
few feet from the alcove accommodating the rock
group, and the lead vocalist appeared to be working
himself into a frenzy. Beckoning a perspiring waiter,
Peter paid the bill.

'Shall we go?' he suggested, leaning towards her a
little. 'Or perhaps you're enjoying yourself too
much?'

Outside, in the dark street, Catriona inhaled great
gulps of night air, and when they reached the car she
leant against it for a moment. The Count opened the
door for her, and when he had climbed in beside her
they sat for a short while in silence.

'I know what you're trying to prove,' she said at
last, 'but it doesn't make any difference. Antoinette
isn't that sort of girl. Even if she went to a place like

that, it wouldn't do anything to her. She'd just be amused by it—you must see that. She's your sister.'

'No, I do not see it.' He started the engine, and they moved slowly forward. 'I see only that she is young, that she is a little foolish. In that kind of atmosphere—' he moved his shoulders expressively, 'she would be just like the others.'

She turned to look at him, startled by a new note in his voice.

'You saw the girl who was drunk?' he asked.

'Yes, but. . . .'

'And you saw her companion?'

'Yes.'

'That was a cousin of Vittorio Falzon.' He put his foot down, and the car began to gather speed. 'Now perhaps you understand.'

Catriona said nothing for several minutes. Whatever the dubious temptations confronting Toni, she still was not convinced that ruthless supervision could be the answer.

'Vittorio may be different,' she said at last. 'And anyway, she has to grow up. You can't shelter her for ever. She has to cope with life, and—and with people. As they are.' She stopped, searching for the right words. 'For one thing . . . it's frightening when someone is too innocent, too vulnerable. Life isn't easy, most people get hurt sooner or later. And when that happens you need to be strong.'

There was silence between them. She waited for his response, but it didn't come, and at last she turned to look at him. By the light of passing street lamps she could see that his face was set. She noticed that he was driving rather fast. She also noticed that they did not seem to be heading back the way they had come.

The Count's left hand moved, extracting a cassette from the small rack beneath the dashboard, and as he slipped it into the deck a harsh, strident sound filled the car. Catriona recognised a symphony by Shosta-kovitch, and she wondered if it were her companion's favourite kind of music or if it just happened to suit his present mood. Possibly he just wanted to put an end to all likelihood of further conversation.

She found herself watching him, the grip of his strong fingers on the steering-wheel, the oddly boyish way his black hair waved, and she wished suddenly that she understood him better. There was a tight-ness in the lines around his mouth, a fixed look about his face. She had a feeling, somehow, that she had upset him, but she wasn't sure how she had done so. Was it because she had referred to the fact that people could so easily be hurt? She felt unsure of her-self suddenly. He bewildered her. She had never known anyone like him.

Ten minutes later she saw that they had at last left the suburbs behind them. They seemed to be follow-ing a series of winding lanes. The lanes were bounded on either side by drystone walls, and beyond the walls she could just make out an uneven landscape of small, stony fields. There was no moon, but to-night the sky was ablaze with the biggest stars she had ever seen.

After a time they emerged on to a different sort of road, and here there were no more walls. She leant forward, peering through the windscreen, and saw that the road seemed to be running across an open cliff-top. In fact, the edge was just a few feet away, and she could even see the sea, a long way below, gleaming like pearl grey silk in the starlight. Moving off the road a little the car stopped, and at the same moment the Count pressed a button, silencing Shostakovitch. Catriona looked at the nearness of the cliff edge and felt a faint stirring of uneasiness. And then that sensation was swallowed up in a different kind of feeling.

The man beside her seemed very close, an overwhelming, intensely masculine presence. She didn't . . . it couldn't be that she found him attractive, but it was strangely difficult not to be aware of him. He was staring fixedly in front of him, deep in thought, and once again she thought how long and thick his eyelashes were. There was a look in his face that made her certain he was going through some sort of torment, and it shook her a little. He seemed to have forgotten her very existence, and she supposed she ought to feel either alarmed or resentful, but she didn't. Instead, she felt a great uprush of sympathy. All at once she wanted more than anything to say something that would reach him, that would break through the barrier of his reserve and soothe the pain of—whatever it was. But she couldn't do that. She didn't know what his problem was, and anyway, it was no concern of hers. Suddenly he opened the car door, and without a word he got out.

She saw him walk to the edge of the cliff, and as he stood, inches from the edge, gazing into the night, a shock ran through her. For a few seconds she hesitated, then she opened the door and went to join him.

The cliff-top grass was thin and dry, scorched by the sun, and the ground felt hard beneath her feet. When she drew close to the edge her nostrils picked up the scent of seaweed, and she could hear the faint murmur of the night tide. She was not afraid of heights, but as she stood beside Peter Vilhena it was a shock to realise that the beach lay hundreds of feet below.

She looked up at Peter, at the rigid lines of his face, and bit her lip, conscious of the fact that she had to say something.

'There must be a wonderful view from here,' she ventured quietly. 'In daylight.'

Slowly she felt him become conscious of her presence beside him and he turned his head to look down at her. Though she couldn't read the expression in his eyes she felt that he was studying her as if he hadn't seen her before, almost as if he had forgotten who she was.

'I'm sorry,' he said abruptly. 'I didn't mean to bring you here.'

'Why not? It looks as if it could be beautiful.'

'Beautiful, yes . . . as you say, in daylight. Everything looks better when the sun has risen.'

Catriona stepped back a little, and he looked at her curiously.

'Have I frightened you?' he asked.

She shook her head. 'No.'

'Good.' His voice was almost gentle. 'I didn't intend to. I needed some air, that's all.'

He turned and drew her back towards the car, and when she was back in her seat he climbed in beside her. Then, just as he was about to start the engine, he glanced at her sharply. 'You're shivering,' he said. 'Why?'

'I . . . I'm cold,' she murmured untruthfully. Why couldn't he leave her alone? Those moments out there on the cliff-top had triggered off a strange reaction in the depths of her being, and she didn't understand it. Nervously, she put a hand up to her face, and in the faint glow from the dashboard light she saw his eyes fasten on her wrist, bruised earlier in the day by the grip of his own fingers.

'I hurt you,' he said quietly, staring at the slim wrist as if it fascinated him.

'It doesn't matter.'

'Yes, it does.' Leaning closer to her, he touched the bruise with one long brown finger. 'I am not usually so violent.'

She felt his warm breath on her cheek, and slowly she turned her head. She met his brilliant brown eyes, and strange little shivers began running through her body. Very gently, his fingers caressed her wrist.

When he kissed her, she remained passive and motionless, almost as if her will had been undermined by some kind of enchantment. His lips were cool, and they lingered only briefly on hers, but in some strange way they took possession of her, mind and body, and when they were withdrawn she felt lost and helpless, as if she had been through a traumatic experience for which she had not been prepared.

'We had better go,' Peter Vilhena said. Without looking at her, he added, 'I'm sorry. That shouldn't have happened.' He started the car, and swinging round in a circle they headed back towards Valletta, leaving the quiet sea behind them.

CHAPTER SEVEN

THE following morning Catriona forced herself to put in an hour's work on her painting of Grand Harbour. Sooner or later—certainly before the picture was finished—she could need to re-visit the Barracça Gardens, but it might be some time before that was possible, and there was a lot that could be done in the privacy of her own room. Besides, she wanted to occupy her mind. She felt a strong disinclination to dwell on the events of the previous evening.

Her painting kept her busy until well past ten o'clock, and it was only when she became intensely conscious of the silence all around her that she realised she ought to go in search of Toni. Taking her courage in both hands, she put her colours away and went downstairs. The house felt quiet and deserted, and she was glad of that, for she didn't particularly want to come face to face with Peter—not just yet. But in the courtyard, reclining on a chaise-longue, she found a slim, tanned figure in a sunshine yellow bikini. Toni, who looked extremely composed, was coating her elegant limbs with sun-tan oil, and at sight of Catriona she smiled widely.

'I am being very lazy,' she remarked with satisfaction. 'Why don't you get into your bikini?'

'Perhaps I will, later on.' Catriona seated herself in a basket-chair, and tried to conceal the fact that she felt slightly taken aback. She had imagined it would be necessary to spend half the morning coaxing Toni into a more cheerful frame of mind, but no such effort appeared to be required.

'Did you have a nice time last night?' Toni was inspecting a damaged fingernail with critical interest.

Catriona started. 'Last night?'

'When you went out with Peter.'

'Oh! It . . . it was interesting.' She felt a ridiculous embarrassment taking possession of her. 'He thought . . . if we had supp— —gether it might help to clear things up,' she ex—   rather lamely.

Toni turned on t— —stomach. 'And did it?'

'I think I may be beginning to understand him.'

'M'mmm. . . . Well, I suppose he is attractive.'

'I didn't—that's not what I meant.' Recollection swept over her, and she tried without much success to prevent herself flushing. 'I . . . I just understand his anxiety a bit better.'

'Well, he doesn't have to worry. I'm going to be a really good girl.' Turning her head a little, Toni nodded towards the plastic bottle on the table beside her. 'Put some oil on my back, would you?'

Slowly, Catriona obeyed. With the bottle in one hand, she looked down at her charge. 'What did you say?' she asked.

'I said I'm going to be a good girl. I won't give him any more trouble, that's all. It isn't worth it. If I behave he won't bother me, and I can still have a lot of fun. All I've got to do is avoid getting seriously involved, and I'm too young for that, anyway. I don't want to muddle my life up. Falling in love isn't for me. Not yet.'

'Well, that sounds sensible.' Catriona eyed her thoughtfully. 'You've done a lot of growing up—since last night.'

'Maybe I have.' Toni sighed. 'I suppose I just suddenly got things into perspective. I don't want to keep struggling, I want to have fun.' She glanced up at Catriona. 'You, too . . . you should be enjoying yourself. Don't worry about me, I'll be fine.' She closed her eyes. 'Thanks for doing my back.'

Catriona found it difficult to understand quite such a dramatic change of attitude, but when she came to think about it she supposed it made sense. After all, Toni was very young. She simply wanted to enjoy herself, to relax and have fun on the sunny island of her ancestors, and she would be perfectly free to do that, as long as she didn't annoy her stepbrother by getting too serious about a boy he didn't like. Presumably, the same taboo would not apply to every male on the island, and in time she might even hit on someone who would meet with the Count's approval. Catriona was surprised, because she wouldn't have expected the other girl to capitulate so easily, or to exhibit so much sound, unromantic sense. But then she didn't know Toni very well. Getting to know people could take time.

Settling herself in a large basket-chair, she stared absently at the sparkling waters of the fountain. She didn't want to keep remembering what had happened the night before, but her mind refused to stop dwelling on it. Of course, he had kissed her on impulse. Even men like Peter Vilhena must occasionally act on impulse, and there wasn't much doubt that he had regretted it immediately. What had he said? 'I'm sorry. That shouldn't have happened.' Catriona had experienced casual kisses before, and naturally it hadn't meant anything to her either. Why should Peter's kiss mean anything?

She stared upwards through a network of orange branches at the hard blue of the sky. Fiercely she told herself that of course Peter's kiss had meant nothing. He had obviously been troubled, the night before, and though she couldn't even begin to guess what his burden was she had felt a tremendous uprush of sympathy. She had been shaken by the strength of her own feelings. A lot had happened during the last day or so, and she had been in a tense, emotional mood— a mood in which it was easy to be affected by other people's problems. As for the kiss—well, that was best forgotten. He would certainly have forgotten it by now, and she didn't want him to guess that she had not.

During the drive back to Valletta they had barely spoken to one another, and it would probably be best, now, if their relationship were kept on as formal a basis as possible.

That evening the Count was out, as he had been all day, and the two girls dined alone. It was intensely hot, and Catriona, who felt rather limp, toyed half-heartedly with a lavish menu which included iced cucumber soup followed by fricassée of veal. At the sight of meringues in hot chocolate sauce, which apparently was the cook's speciality, she gave up altogether, and soon afterwards was able to make her escape, going up to her room for an early night. But not before Toni, who was in high spirits, had come to a decision that the following day they would go for a drive around the Island.

Catriona, she pointed out, had not really seen Malta yet, and that was a situation which had to be remedied. Besides, it was time they left the stifling atmosphere of the capital behind them, even if it were only for an hour or two. She herself didn't drive, but Mario would take them. It would not be difficult to arrange.

Shortly after nine in the morning they set out, having been given permission to use the big Citroën, and as she relaxed in the back Catriona wondered how the Count felt about parting with his favourite car for the space of a whole day. She knew that he had others, but the Citroën was undoubtedly the one he used most frequently. Toni's request for a car had been made through Mario, so it would have been difficult to discover exactly how he had reacted, and in any case Catriona was anxious not to betray too much curiosity. She had not seen him since the night she had had supper with him, and she didn't think Toni had.

As they climbed out of Valletta and emerged on to the coast road it was already fiercely hot, and she didn't feel very much like sightseeing. But Malta, she discovered, was an interesting island, and on the whole she enjoyed the day's expedition. To begin with, they made their way along a road that clung to the Mediterranean, and she would never have believed that water could be so intensely blue. Here, there were no cliffs, simply a low, rocky shoreline and a cautious enquiry elicited information which suggested that Peter must have taken her to the other side of the Island. She saw nothing to remind her of the disturbing incident at the cliff edge, and after a time she was able to relax and enjoy the brilliance of the Mediterranean morning.

Near St. Paul's Bay, a sprawling modern resort marking the spot that once witnessed the shipwreck of St. Paul, they turned inland, and Catriona wondered why, from the air, the whole island had looked so bleak and barren. The roads were very dusty, and the small, carefully cultivated fields were often parched, but in the : 'and villages children played in the shade of spreading carob trees, and there were olive groves on the terraced slopes. There were ancient pine trees, too, and behind high walls she caught glimpses of bright, exotic gardens.

They had lunch in Mdina, the old, walled capital at the centre of the Island, and over her fried chicken Toni smiled.

'M'mm! I am enjoying myself, I think.'

Catriona smiled. 'So am I. Malta's a beautiful place.'

After lunch they wandered through the streets of the old town, and Catriona felt as if she had been whisked back through four centuries of time. Mdina, she learned, had always been known as the Silent City, and it was easy to understand why. A great stillness prevailed within the ancient walls, and in the shadowed streets there was hardly any movement. Majestic, fairy-tale palaces crowded close to one another, and romantic stone staircases wound upwards towards massive fifteenth-century ramparts. Valletta had been the City of the Knights, but Mdina had been the home of the Maltese nobility, and a faint hauteur still clung to its time-worn stones.

They were just beginning to make their way back to the car, which had been left in the Cathedral square, when they passed an ancient arched doorway, and from its recesses an only too familiar voice addressed them. Both girls jumped.

'Well . . . ! I am glad to see that you are employing yourselves profitably. The Silent City always repays study.'

Recovering her composure, Toni looked mildly irritated. 'I didn't know you would be here.'

'As you see, I am about to call upon Zia Elena. I do occasionally visit my relations.'

Toni pouted. 'You didn't tell me.'

'I didn't think you would be interested. However, since you are evidently in a dutiful mood I am sure she would be delighted to see you.' For the first time, the Count looked directly at Catriona. 'You, too, Miss Browne. I have no doubt that my great-aunt would be happy to make your acquaintance.'

Catriona felt as if her mouth had gone dry. She had imagined him to be several miles away, in Valletta, and at the unexpected encounter, her pulses had begun to throb. She drew back a little.

'No—oh, no, I wouldn't dream of butting in. I'll go and look round the museum. And . . . and the Cathedral. . . .'

'Don't be silly.' Toni placed slender fingers on her arm, detaining her. 'You must come and see my aunt. She's a darling old lady, nearly ninety, and tougher than I am. Isn't she, Peter?'

'That is not a particularly respectful description, but it comes close to the truth.' He tugged at an elaborate iron chain, and a series of bells began to clamour in the stillness behind the massive oak door.

The door was opened, eventually, by an elderly maid clad in rusty black, and after a brief interchange they were all admitted to the house. The maid had evidently been expecting Count Vilhena, but she had not anticipated being required to receive the rest of the party, and it was clear that she didn't particularly like such a large-scale invasion. To Catriona's embarrassment, she eyed both young women with a marked lack of enthusiasm, and it seemed probable that if she had not held the Count in considerable esteem she might even have asked them to leave. As it was, she muttered irritably in Maltese, and held her shoulders stiffly as she led the way up a magnificent stone staircase to the first-floor *salotto* where the Countess Cicogna was waiting to receive her nephew.

The *salotto* turned out to be immensely long and its solitary occupant looked very small as she sat, bolt upright, in a straight-backed Florentine chair. She was wearing a well-cut grey silk dress, and her thick white hair had been coiled expertly about her head. There were some wonderful pearls at her wrinkled throat, and an emerald blazed on her right hand.

'Good afternoon, madame.' Bending towards her, Peter lifted one of the small, ring-laden hands and kissed it. Then he leant forward and dropped a second kiss on her cheek. 'You are well?'

'Of course I am well.' Her piercing black eyes scanned his face. 'You are just back from England? Why must you always work so hard? It's not necessary, Pietru.'

'I don't work hard, madame.' He had been holding the old lady's hand in both his own, but now, gently, he returned it to her lap. 'As you know, I do no more than I am obliged to do.'

She looked past him, and her bird-like glance fell on the two girls. At sight of Toni her eyes brightened, then they settled for a long moment on Catriona.

'You are not alone, I see. You bring my little Antoinette. Come and kiss me, child.'

Toni ran forward and placed an arm about the bony, silk-clad shoulders. 'You are pleased to see me, madame?'

'Yes, child, of course. Though you should not wear so much make-up, and that perfume is too strong.' For the second time, she focussed her attention on Catriona. 'Peter, who is this?'

He drew Catriona forward. 'This is Miss Browne, madame. She comes from England. She is giving Antoinette the benefit of her companionship.'

'Ah, a companion!' The old eyebrows puckered. 'Does she like being a companion?'

'I really could not say, madame.' His tone was suave. 'You must ask Miss Browne.'

Catriona flushed, and returned the Countess's gaze with as much composure as she could muster. 'I like Malta very much,' she said quietly. 'I'm lucky to have been given such an opportunity.'

'That does not answer my question,' the old lady returned dryly. 'Still, I forgive you. And I am sure you understand that nothing in this world is really a question of "luck". You are in Malta because you were destined to come here, that is quite certain. Now, come and sit beside me.' She indicated a low, embroidered stool. 'Tell me about England. I was there in 1932, just before I got married for the second time. I stayed in London, and noticed that the theatre had become very improper. Tell me. . . .'

She embarked on a long series of questions and Catriona, sitting next to her, tried hard to provide suitably intelligent answers. Toni joined in with enthusiasm, for she considered herself to be quite an authority on England, but the Count seated himself a short distance away, detaching himself from the conversation. When Catriona looked towards him she found his eyes upon her. There was an inscrutable look upon his face. For a moment she held his glance, before turning away, unable to control a heightening of her colour.

After a while the maid reappeared, bearing a large silver tray laden with delicate china, and to her surprise Catriona discovered that they were to be served with afternoon tea. The Countess, it seemed, had as a young woman acquired the habit of drinking afternoon tea, when it had been fashionable among her contemporaries to adopt English social customs, and she was proud of the fact that she had kept the tradition going. Manipulating a heavy silver teapot with skill, she remarked sternly that insularity was a crime.

'In other people's countries one finds much that is good,' she informed her guests. 'We must keep open minds and open hearts.'

During tea, Peter Vilhena moved closer to his great-aunt, and she bombarded him ruthlessly with penetrating questions, most of them concerned with details of his everyday life. He responded skilfully, sometimes clearly resorting to a little discreet evasion, sometimes allowing himself to be disarmingly honest.

When the tea-tray was finally removed it was a sign that the interview was over, and they all stood up. The Countess, a little tired, lay back against her embroidered cushions.

'For me,' she said, 'this has been a happy afternoon. Peter, you will bring these children to see me again?'

He bowed. 'At any time you wish, Aunt Elena.'

Toni rushed impulsively over to kiss the sallow

cheek. 'I'll come as often as you like.' she promised
unexpectedly.

'Good, I am glad.' The old lady patted Toni's
hand, and then she looked round quickly, her eyes
searching for Catriona. 'You will come too, Miss
Browne?' She held out her free hand to the English
girl. 'We must talk again—of London, and the South
Downs, and the moors that you like so much. And
you must show me one of your paintings.'

Catriona took her hand, smiling uncertainly.
'Thank you, madame, I'd like to come again.'

The bright old eyes studied her keenly, the bony
fingers squeezed hers with surprising energy, and
then they dropped back into their owner's lap. A
door was opened by the maid and the Countess's
visitors filed out, down the Romeo and Juliet staircase to the dim, marble-floored hall.

'Where is Mario?' the Count wanted to know. He
seemed to be addressing his stepsister, but his eyes
were on Catriona.

'M'mm, he's around somewhere. Having a nap, I
suppose. We'll find him.' Toni glanced at the English girl. 'Come on, Catriona, let's go and do some
exploring.'

The front door was being held open for them, and
once again they ventured out into the fierce heat of
the afternoon. As they crossed the threshold Toni
glanced back, casually, at the man behind them.

'See you later, Peter!'

Catriona didn't hear him reply, and she hadn't the
courage to look at him again.

They retraced their steps along the street, and
after a minute or two emerged into the Cathedral
square. Toni yawned loudly, and at sight of the

parked Citroën heaved a dramatic sigh of relief.

'Thank goodness, there's Mario. Let's get away from this place—I've had enough of Mdina.'

'I thought you wanted to do some exploring.'

Toni made a face. 'Exploring? Heavens, not in this heat. You don't want to, do you?'

They were inside the car, and doors were being closed on them. Catriona shook her head slowly.

'No, I don't. I just wondered. . . .'

'You wondered why I did not tell Peter the truth? Well, we had to get rid of him, didn't we? If I hadn't said that, he might have come with us.'

'Yes, I suppose he might.'

Toni looked at her sharply, then lapsed into a thoughtful silence which lasted all the way back to Valletta.

They spent the following morning exploring churches, museums and galleries. In the magnificent Cathedral of St John, Catriona stood spellbound before glowing frescos and tapestries, and in the beautiful crypt she lingered by the tomb of La Valette. When they reached the National Museum she was intrigued by a large collection of Stone Age relics, and she made the discovery that Malta was of surprising importance to students of pre-history. Mysterious 'cart-tracks', embedded in stone, had been discovered on the island, and there were several great Neolithic temples, reminiscent of England's Stonehenge. During the afternoon they visited one of the temples, a majestic, frightening place overlooking the dark brilliance of the sea, and Catriona, disturbed and fascinated, would have liked to linger among the massive ruins, watching as the sun went down. She longed for an opportunity to commit the scene to canvas, and hoped that the following day she would be able, alone, to make her way back.

Toni was good company, but she always seemed a little abstracted, and she obviously found it difficult to share the English girl's enthusiasm for antiquities. Sitting on a fallen stone, she waited with as much patience as she could muster while Catriona inspected the ruins of Hagiar Qim, but at half past six she looked at her watch and observed plantively that it really was time they thought about getting back to Valletta.

'We are going to a party to-night. I told you, remember?'

'A party?' Catriona glanced at her, slightly startled. 'I'm sorry, I'm afraid I don't remember.'

'It's one of my girl friends—her nineteenth birthday. She specially wanted you to be there. I *told* you.'

'Oh!' For some reason, Catriona didn't feel in the least like sampling the Maltese social scene. 'Wouldn't you rather go by yourself?' she suggested hopefully. 'I mean . . . I expect you'll know everybody there.'

Toni looked hurt and surprised. 'But I thought you would like to come!' In a small voice, she added: 'Peter will not like it if I go alone.'

She was right, of course, Catriona realised that. And strictly speaking, it was her job to go. If she didn't, there wasn't much doubt that Peter Vilhena would regard the omission as a dereliction of duty.

'All right. If you really want me to go with you.'

Toni jumped up, as pleased and gratified as a child. 'Of course I do! It will be such fun. I can't wait to hear what you think of everybody.'

They set out to walk back through the ruins, and

Catriona smiled a little ruefully at the other girl. 'I'm sorry I dragged you over here this afternoon. I must seem a bore.'

'Oh, no, you could never be a bore! But you're clever, and I'm not. It's interesting, knowing someone who is really clever.' As they walked towards the car, Toni stole a sideways glance at Catriona. 'Do you think Peter has noticed?' she asked.

'Noticed what?'

'How clever you are.'

Catriona flushed. For some absurd reason the remark irritated her.

'I'm not in the least clever,' she responded crisply. 'And if I were, I'm quite sure your brother wouldn't notice.'

They got back to Valletta just before seven o'clock and half an hour later were ready to set out. As she dressed, slipping into her new embroidered skirt and the silk top that went with it, Catriona found herself hoping they would not bump into Peter, and when they succeeded in driving away without encountering a soul apart from Carmen she ought to have been relieved. But somehow she felt a little flat. She also felt very plain and ordinary beside Toni, who was exotically beautiful in kingfisher blue.

The party was being held in a large, sprawling modern villa perched on a hill above Sliema, and it was obviously very much a get-together for the children of the aristocracy. Most of the young men were wearing immaculate dinner-jackets, and the girls' dresses bore the stamp of London, Paris and New York. They all spoke excellent English, and they seemed to have a slightly feverish capacity for enjoyment.

On a long terrace overlooking the dark line of the sea a small local band was playing country style music, which apparently was popular on the island. By the time Catriona arrived with Toni quite a few couples were already dancing. A dozen or so more were sipping champagne in a large, exotically furnished room behind the terrace, and the nineteen-year-old hostess was amongst them. Gina Sciberras was small, dark and beautiful, like a figure from the Arabian Nights, and she was the centre of an admiring circle, predominantly male. There wasn't much doubt that she was enjoying herself.

At sight of Toni, however, she broke away from the group and hurried forward to greet her friend. For a few moments they spoke rapidly in Maltese, and then Gina held out a slender brown hand to Toni's English companion.

'Catriona, I am so happy that you could come! You have done a lot, I think, for Antoinette. You like Malta?'

'I love it,' Catriona told her, realising as she spoke that it was the truth.

The Maltese girl smiled brilliantly, and looking around caught sight of a solid young man in spectacles.

'Anton, come and talk to Catriona. She has travelled all the way from England, and you must look after her for me.'

Anton approached, smiling eagerly if a little shortsightedly at the slight figure of the English girl. 'Good evening!' He bowed. 'You have just arrived, *signurina*?'

'No. Actually, I've been here for several days.' She looked around, and made the discovery that Toni had vanished, together with their hostess.

Anton procured her a glass of something innocuous, and they went out on to the terrace. He wasn't in the least attractive, but she had to talk to someone, and she wasn't at all in the mood for romantic encounters. They began to dance, slowly, to a ballad that had started life in Tennessee, and looking around for Toni Catriona caught a glimmer of kingfisher blue at the far end of the terrace. Well, at least her charge was still in sight, and that really ought to be enough. Toni, after all, was a little bit old for needing a nanny.

Slightly out of breath, Anton stepped on one of her toes, and apologised. He was shorter than she was, and as he beamed up at her through his rimless spectacles he reminded her irresistibly of a rare species of owl, once encountered while bird-watching with her grandfather in the vicinity of the Norfolk Broads. Resolutely, she pushed the idea out of her mind and forced herself to listen to his conversation.

'I am not a good dancer, I don't have much time. You see, I'm studying hard.'

'Oh? What are you studying?'

'I am going to be an architect, which is very hard work.'

'I'm sure it is.'

'You are also studying something?'

'I paint pictures,' Catriona admitted reluctantly, and he uttered a little squeak of enthusiasm, at the same time treading very hard on her right foot.

'You paint pictures?' Through the spectacles his round brown eyes, alight with innocent interest, gazed into hers. 'But this is most fascinating. Please tell me about them.'

To Catriona's relief, the ballad soon came to an end, but it was half an hour before she succeeded in getting away from Anton, and when she did finally make her escape it was only to be seized upon almost immediately by Gina Sciberras' handsome brother, Paolo. He got her another drink, something she would have preferred not to have, and told her eagerly that he had been hearing all about her. Guiding her out on to the terrace, he remarked softly that there were not enough English girls around these days, and almost in the same breath asked if he might have the pleasure of showing her the Island.

'Thanks, I've seen quite a lot of it already, and I'm really here to work.'

'But one does not work all the time. What is your English saying. . . . "*All work and no play makes—makes——*"'

' "*Jack a dull boy*",' she supplied helpfully.

'But it is not possible for you to be a boy.' Laughing with considerable satisfaction at his own joke, he steered her out among the dancers, now writhing to the insistent beat of a current hit. They danced together several times, then Catriona settled herself on a pile of cushions while Paolo plied her with dainties from the nearby buffet.

For the time being she had resigned herself to his company, partly because there didn't seem to be much chance of losing him, and partly because Gina's brother might be a useful person to have on hand if Toni should actually disappear. She didn't know why, but she had a strange, irrational feeling that the Count's stepsister might be inclined to do exactly that. She glimpsed Toni several times during the evening, but always from a distance. Toni did, it was true, seem to be dancing with several different boys, and that, in itself, was some consolation, for it seemed to indicate that her special friend was not around. It must be that, or she had fallen out with him.

Catriona wasn't quite sure why she was so anxious to behave like a nineteenth-century duenna, and once or twice she told herself firmly that she was being absurd. She didn't even know the boy Toni was so keen on, so why should she want to curb their budding romance? Whatever the Count had said, Catriona couldn't believe, somehow, that there was anything seriously wrong with Vittorio Falzon, and if Toni were on the brink of falling in love, who was she to try and put a stop to it?

But she was haunted by the disapproval in a pair of dark, masculine eyes, and by the memory of Peter Vilhena's voice. She could imagine what he would say to her if Toni's little entanglement got out of hand. He would be angry, because he was so sure it was the wrong thing for Toni, and he might be right.

Anyway, she didn't want him to be angry with her. The sudden realisation hit her as if somebody had slapped her face, and she stood stock still in the middle of the dance floor, seriously upsetting Paolo's execution of a new step. It couldn't be . . . it couldn't really be that she cared what Peter thought of her. She remembered him as he had been when she first saw him in England—his arrogance, his conceit, his indifference to the feelings of other people, and then she thought about his behaviour since her arrival in Malta. He didn't really see her as a human being. To him, she was just an employee, someone who had been engaged to take charge of his stepsister. In an abstracted mood he had driven her up on to the cliffs without even recollecting that she was beside him in the car. Then, for no reason, he had kissed her, thinking obviously of someone else, and that had been the final insult.

Furiously, she bit her lip. What on earth had she been doing all evening? What had made her believe that she had some sort of duty to spy on Toni?

'Sorry,' she said, smiling brilliantly at Paolo. 'I just remembered something, that's all. It wasn't important.'

Two hours later the guests began to disperse and Catriona told Paolo firmly that it was time she thought about going too. Several times during the last hour he had suggested that she might like to go for a reviving walk in the garden, but on some pretext or other she had firmly resisted every such suggestion. Now he looked down at her ruefully.

'You are going so soon? When shall I see you again?'

'I don't know. I'm very busy, really. I have two jobs to do.'

'I shall come and watch you paint.'

She smiled. 'I don't know where I'll be.'

'I'll find you.'

'All right,' she said lightly, 'I'll look out for you. And now I must look for Antoinette.'

'Why? Antoinette can take care of herself.'

'Maybe. But at the moment she's my responsibility, and we have to go.' Catriona glanced round the long room, now nearly empty of people, and made the discovery that Toni was definitely nowhere to be seen. Hurrying to one of the long windows, she looked out across the terrace. A conscientious man-

servant was already extinguishing fairy-lights, and
the band was packing up. Two or three couples were
giggling hysterically near the parapet that overlooked
the lights of Sliema, but Toni wasn't with them, and
Catriona felt sudden panic spreading through her. It
was all very well to have decided not to spy on Toni,
but losing her was quite another matter. Where on
earth could she have got to?

She turned round, to find Paolo close behind her.

'I can't find Antoinette,' she said, her voice clear
and taut with anxiety.

He shrugged. 'Why worry? Maybe one of her boy-
friends took her home.'

'I wasn't supposed to let her out of my sight.' As
soon as the words had left her lips she realised that
they made her sound like a downtrodden Victorian
governess, but it was true, all the same, and she felt
guilty. She was, after all, being paid to do a job, and
she had let her employer down. If she had no intention of earning her salary she ought not to be here,
in Malta, collecting shelter and payment from the
brother of Antoinette Caruana.

She became aware of the fact that Gina was beside
her now, and that she was looking a little anxious.

'You must not worry, Catriona. I am sure she is
safe. Old Mario is waiting to drive you home, and I
expect when you get back to Valletta you will find
her already there.'

'Are you sure she's not here?' Catriona looked
around her with a hint of desperation, almost as if
she suspected the existence of a secret panel.

'Yes, I am sure.' The Maltese girl smiled in what
was meant to be a reassuring manner. 'Perhaps she
was dancing with someone, and—and it was so hot

this evening. He may have said "Let's go for a drive. . . ." '

'Well, who would it have been, do you think?'

'Who knows?' Gina shrugged a little uneasily.

Feeling angry and frustrated, Catriona hesitated. It would be so simple just to ask about Vittorio Falzon—to find out whether he had been among the guests. Yet she couldn't do anything of the kind without revealing that she knew of a link between Vittorio and Toni, and that would involve the betrayal of a confidence.

She looked from Gina to her brother, and back again. 'Well, thanks for a lovely evening. I suppose I'd better just go back to Valletta and see what happens.'

Paolo accompanied her to the small gravelled area where cars had been left, and she tried not to sound impatient as she dealt with his repeated enquiries about the possibility of seeing her again soon. Mario had probably spent part of the evening, at least, in the kitchens of the Villa, but he was now back in the Citroën's driving seat, and as Catriona approached he sprang out smartly to open a door for her.

'Mario,' she asked, 'have you see Miss Antoinette?'

He stroked his bare grey head. 'No, *signurina*.'

'They say she may have let someone take her home, but perhaps we ought not to go until we're sure.'

He shrugged. 'If she is not here, then she has gone home, *signurina*.'

Catriona hoped sincerely that he was right. She climbed into the car, and reluctantly Paolo closed the door on her. Smoothly they swung out of the car park and into the tortuous streets of old Sliema, and ten minutes later they were back at Palazzo Vilhena.

A lantern burned above the front entrance, but otherwise the whole building appeared to be in darkness, possibly because most of the windows were shuttered. Catriona sprang out of the car, hurriedly thanking Mario, but when she tried to open the massive door she discovered, as she might have expected, that it was locked.

Still hovering, Mario indicated an electric bell. 'You must ring, *signurina*.'

She did so, and a few moments later the door swung inwards, opened by Carmen. Thankfully, Catriona said goodnight to Mario and stepped inside.

In the darkened passageway she gazed anxiously at the maid. 'Miss Antoinette—has she come back yet?'

'*Iva, signurina*, half an hour ago. She asked me to get her a cup of chocolate, and then she went to bed.' Carmen looked curious. 'You had a nice evening, *signurina*? Can I get you something?'

'No, thank you.' Catriona felt swamped by the relief surging over her. 'I'll—I'll be going up to bed, too. Goodnight, Carmen.'

'Goodnight, *signurina*.'

Too discreet to betray any further curiosity, the maid melted away, leaving Catriona alone. The lamp beneath the image of the Virgin burned very brightly now, and its glow was somehow comforting. She leant against the door, feeling herself relax.

How stupid she had been! Probably Toni had had a headache, and rather than spoil the evening for her English friend she had just asked someone to drive her home quietly. It could easily have been as simple as that.

Poor Toni.

Giving herself a little shake, Catriona began to move towards the doorway leading to the long hall. Then, abruptly, a door on the other side of the passage opened. It was the door leading to the Count's inner sanctum, and it was Peter himself who was standing on the threshold.

CHAPTER EIGHT

Count Vilhena stood watching her in the glow cast by the tiny lamp. 'Good evening,' he said at last.

'Good evening.' Catriona felt awkward, guilty, like a schoolgirl caught creeping in after 'lights out'.

'I am glad to see that Mario brought you home safely. You have just got in?'

'Yes.' When, she wondered, was he going to start making enquiries about Toni?

He was still studying her, and though his face was in shadow she could feel the disapproval in his eyes. 'Antoinette came in half an hour ago,' he told her suddenly. 'I understand she was brought back by a friend. Someone she played with as a child.'

Catriona turned towards him. 'I'm sorry,' she began. 'I didn't intend—I really meant to keep an eye on her.'

He bowed slightly. 'I am sure you did. She came to no harm, in any case. I was not too worried about the Sciberras' party. They are an excellent family— my father knew them well. When Gina and Paolo entertain there is always, I believe, discreet supervision.'

Catriona could not remember noticing anything suggestive of parental surveillance, but the evening had certainly been well organised.

'It was a very nice party,' she said at last. In spite of the fact that Toni seemed to be in the clear, disapproval was still there, strong in his voice, and it made her feel uneasy.

'So I understand. At least, I am told that you found it enjoyable. When Antoinette left, apparently, you were having what she terms a "good time".'

'Oh! But I wasn't, really. I mean. . . .' She flushed. 'It wasn't quite my kind of party.'

'Ah! And what is your kind of party?' There was a note of interest in his voice which she had never heard before.

'I don't know, really. I like to talk, and listen to music.'

'You don't like to dance?'

'Yes, sometimes, but I suppose it depends mainly on the people you're with. That kind of thing.'

'I see.' He raised his eyebrows. 'And you didn't like the people you were with to-night?'

'I didn't mean that.' What on earth was the matter with her? Why couldn't she just say something non-committal? Why, with him, did she always have to be so awkward?

'You certainly sound rather flat,' he observed dryly. 'We shall have to find some sort of entertain-ment that appeals to you.'

'The party was fun. I'm just a bit tired, that's all.' She took a step forward, and was about to say 'good-night' when he spoke again.

'Come and have coffee with me.'

Catriona hesitated. A pulse at the base of her throat began to throb, and she moistened her lips.

'It's rather late, isn't it?'

'Yes, but I'd like to talk to you.'

She swallowed, trying to curb an absurd sensation of panic. Obviously, he was in a relaxed mood which she had never known with him before. With an

effort, she forced herself to say calmly: 'Thanks, I . . .
I'd like a coffee.'

'Good.' He stood aside, and she walked past him
into the small, square room that he used as an office.
As usual, the desk was littered with papers, and he
seemed to have been working hard. Seeing him now,
in a stronger light, she realised that he looked tired.

For the first time she noticed that there was a large
oil painting on the wall above the desk, and she went
over to study it more closely. The picture showed a
small yacht, all sails set, driven before the wind and
riding the crest of a wave. Behind, a great expanse of
sky blazed with stormy light, and there was no land
to be seen.

He walked over to the bell and pressed it. 'The
painting interests you?' he asked.

She nodded, slowly. 'Yes, it's remarkable. Do you
know who the artist was? There's no signature.'

'The artist is dead,' he said shortly.

Catriona didn't understand the note in his voice,
and when she turned to look at him she was puzzled
by the tightness about his mouth. She wanted to ask
more about the painting, but every instinct told her
that it would be better not to do so.

When Carmen appeared he asked her to bring
coffee, and as she left the room he once again directed
his cool stare at Catriona.

'Sit down.' He gestured towards the only comfort-
able-looking chair in the room, a wicker rocking-
chair that looked as if it might have been made on
the island.

She obeyed, but instantly regretted doing so, for
he remained standing and she felt at a ridiculous dis-
advantage.

'You look rather apprehensive,' he observed. 'Or at least, you did when you came in just now.'

She tried to laugh. 'I'm not apprehensive. Why should I be?'

'I can't answer that. I just feel that you have a tendency to regard me as a gazelle regards a prowling lion.'

'I don't see myself as a gazelle.'

'I don't see myself as a prowling lion, but the rest of the world tends to think differently, sometimes.'

When Carmen returned he instructed her to place the small silver coffee tray beside Catriona, and after the maid had gone he suggested that she should pour out. As she did so, she recollected that it was not the first time she had poured coffee in front of him. She remembered that evening at the Calverley Hotel.

She saw him give a slight smile. 'I hope,' he said, 'you're not going to pour it over me.'

'That's not fair,' she protested, filling her own cup with fingers that, in spite of her efforts, refused to steady themselves.

'Nevertheless, I do seem to have the most unfortunate effect on your approach to a coffee-pot.' He sat down on a corner of the desk. 'So you don't like noisy parties. What do you like?'

'I thought I told you,' she said. The coffee was strong and stimulating, and as she sipped it she felt better.

'I think you described the kind of social gathering you find congenial, but that's not quite what I'm talking about. You say you are fond of people, conversation . . . music. Do you find that these things make life worth while?'

'Not by themselves. Of course not.'

'So what does, in your estimation?'

'That's a big question.'

'Yes. But you see, I'm curious about you. So strong, so independent.' He turned and glanced at the painting behind him. 'As you will have noticed, that yacht is struggling against heavy seas. Wind, water—everything is against her. Human life is like that, don't you agree?'

'I suppose it is, a bit,' Catriona answered cautiously. 'Though it's true that for some people the weather always seems to be calm.'

'Yes,' he nodded. 'But you are not one of those people, I think. You are always prepared. Your defences are carefully co-ordinated. You are braced against the storm.'

There was silence for several seconds.

'That sounds dreadful,' she said, trying to speak lightly. 'I'll have to do something about my image.'

He studied her intently. 'Where are your parents?' he asked.

'My father is dead. My mother's in the Philippines . . . I think. She—married again.'

'I see.' His voice was suddenly soft. 'And how long is it since you were left to fend entirely for yourself?'

'Not very long. I stayed at school until I was eighteen, you see. My grandparents' trust fund paid for that.'

'How old were you when your father died and your mother remarried?'

He was cross-examining her, but she hadn't the will to protest. Besides, there was a strange gentleness in his voice and in his manner.

'Daddy died when I was fourteen, but my mother was already—they separated two years before that.'

She dragged the words out, her voice husky.

'You were very young when these things happened. Did you not find it hard to carry on?'

Catriona shook her head. 'Not really. Everyone has the strength to carry on, especially when they're young.'

'If we exert strength,' he pointed out, 'it's usually for a purpose.'

She looked at him. 'Well, there always is a purpose. Life itself—that's enough, isn't it?'

'Is it?' he asked. "*Life is very sweet, brother . . . who would wish to die . . .?*" Of course, it was a countryman of yours who wrote those words. But life is not always sweet.'

'Well, when it isn't one just has to have faith,' she said quietly. 'Sometimes, of course, things can seem pretty black, but when that happens you just have to keep putting one foot in front of the other. Then— one day—you look around and realise you've left the bad things right behind you. And sometimes the good things are just coming up over the horizon.'

'What happens if one has lost one's ability to appreciate the good things?'

'I don't believe one ever does. Of course, it's possible to be stunned for a while, but then. . . .' She broke off, embarrassed. 'I don't know why you're asking me all this. I . . . you can't possibly want to know what I think, and it's getting very late. . . .'

She stood up, as she did so absentmindedly gathering up the tray. After a moment, Peter also got to his feet.

'I asked you because I wanted to know.' He took the tray from her and set it down on his desk among the tumbled papers. 'You had better avoid coffeepots in future—they seem to have a strange effect on you. Your hands are trembling again.'

'I'm tired,' she said, avoiding his eyes.

He reached out and took one of her hands. Holding it between both of his own, he began to study the slim, capable fingers, the short, well-manicured nails. A strange feeling ran through her, almost like an electric shock, and her fingers began to tremble in earnest. She snatched them away and quickly, to cover her embarrassment, she mentioned Toni.

'I . . . I think I ought to go and see her. Just for a moment.'

'Antoinette, I should imagine, has been asleep for an hour.'

Catriona forced herself to look up at him, and found herself looking straight into his eyes. They were as dark as the night beyond the windows, black and velvety, and not for the first time she had the uncanny feeling that he could see into the depths of her soul. For a long moment they gazed at one another, and she felt herself held by a magnetic power so strong that she could not bring herself to look away.

Then, somewhere, a clock began chiming twelve, and quite suddenly he turned away. He began to sift through the papers on his desk, and when he did speak his voice was casual.

'Tomorrow morning I shall be going to Gozo. You know where that is?'

'Yes, it's a small island to the north of Malta.'

'That's right, our sister island. By Maltese tradition, the brightest jewel in the crown of the Mediterranean. The crown, of course, being Malta herself.' He frowned abstractedly at a document lying in front of him. 'I have a small boatyard over there, and it's time I carried out a personal tour of inspection. If you like, you could go with me.'

Her eyes opened very wide. She was at a loss for words. 'I'm sure Toni would like that,' she managed at last.

'I did not mention Antoinette.' The frown grew more pronounced as he flicked impatiently through an open file.

'Well——' She felt a little lightheaded. 'Thank you, I'd like to see Gozo. It—it would be fun.'

He didn't look up. 'I think you might enjoy it. I shall be taking a launch across, and we'll leave at half past eight in the morning, so you had better go to bed and get some sleep.'

'Yes, I . . . I will.' With one hand on the door-handle she paused. 'Goodnight. Thanks for the coffee.'

He glanced up, and for a fraction of a second she thought his face softened again. 'Goodnight,' he said Then he bent over his desk, seemingly to put her firmly out of his mind.

Quietly she slipped out of the room. As she climbed the long staircase to her bedroom she thought again that Toni ought to be going with them in the morning. But she didn't worry about it much. She had a strange hazy feeling, as if she had temporarily lost touch with reality—as if she were walking in a dream.

CHAPTER NINE

The following morning she was up very early, when the sun had not long risen and the sky was still streaked with the golden light of dawn. She felt oddly tranquil and relaxed and she dressed slowly, taking time over her bath, washing her hair before slipping into one of the sundresses she had bought a few days before. She used little make-up for she had been in the sun a good deal since her arrival in Malta, and she had already acquired a soft, even tan, but for the protection of her skin she applied foundation and a good sun-cream before brushing the tips of her lashes with mascara and touching her lips with a warm, rosy lipstick.

When she had finished, she studied herself critically in the long mirror beside her bed, and couldn't help feeling a little startled at the sight of her own reflection. Her skin glowed, her eyes were bright, and she looked strangely different from the girl who a few days earlier had been dismissed by the manager of the Calverley Hotel.

At eight o'clock Carmen brought breakfast to her room and she commented enthusiastically on Catriona's dress, which was the colour of English hare-bells.

'It's very beautiful, *signurina*. You look like a princess. Are you going somewhere nice today?'

Her brown eyes were alight with slightly speculative interest and Catriona felt embarrassed. It had obviously not been lost on Carmen that the English girl had been in her employer's study at a late hour the night before, nor would she have been likely to forget that she had been asked to serve them both with coffee.

She tried to smile casually. 'I'm just going out for the day. Over to Gozo.'

'Ah, Gozo! Across the water? You don't mind?'

'Should I? Will it be a rough crossing?'

Carmen shrugged. 'I don't know, but I don't like to go in boats. And sometimes—yes, it's very rough. Sometimes there are storms.' She made a growling noise in her throat, evidently intended to represent a clap of thunder.

Catriona laughed. 'Nothing is likely to happen to-day,' she pointed out. 'It's such beautiful weather.'

The maid looked dubious. 'It's much too hot. Maria! In this weather I have a headache all the time.'

Just before half past eight, Catriona went down-stairs. She found the front door standing open, and in the street outside a smart Renault two-seater was waiting. There was no one inside the car, but an old woman dressed in black was walking past, and she grinned toothily at Catriona.

'*Bon giorn, signurina.*'

Catriona had not yet had time to learn much Maltese, but she understood simple greetings, and she smiled back at the woman. '*Bon giorn,*' she answered swiftly.

Behind her a well-known voice spoke. 'Excellent. Are you planning to take a serious, scholarly interest in our language, or have you just been glancing through a phrase-book?'

Turning to face him, she tensed very slightly, conscious of the fact that he seemed to be teasing her. 'I haven't got a Maltese phrase-book,' she admitted. 'I've just been listening to people.'

'How very sensible.' He was standing still, looking at her, and she began to feel selfconscious. 'That colour,' he said after a moment. 'What do you call it?'

She realised that he meant the colour of her dress. 'It's—well, it's a sort of misty blue.'

'You should wear it often,' he said coolly. 'But as an artist you probably know that already.' Briskly, he opened the car door for her. 'You have strong sunglasses?' he asked, looking down at her.

'Yes, they're Polaroid.' She hesitated. 'My eyes are important to me, and I tend to look after them.'

'I'm glad to hear it.' He went round and slipped behind the steering wheel. 'At sea you will find that the light is very strong.'

He was wearing a white shirt, open at the neck, and its short sleeves revealed the muscular strength of his tanned arms. She realised that his body had a look of controlled power, usually associated with professional athletes, and she wondered how he managed to stay so fit.

Within a few minutes they had left Valletta behind them, and a short time later they were out on the winding coast road. Already the heat was fierce, and Catriona felt her shoulders burning. On their right, the sea was a harsh line of cobalt blue, but to the left there was nothing but rough scrubland, bare and blistered like the surface of the moon. She knew that they were heading for Marsa, a small harbour at the northern tip of the island. She understood that the drive would probably take them something like half an hour.

He said very little during the journey, but it didn't matter. For the first time she didn't feel that his silence was intended to convey hostility.

They passed small, weatherbeaten watch-towers, originally built as part of the island's defences against possible Turkish invasion. Once, the square keep of a mediaeval castle loomed up beside them, blotting out the sun. After a time they reached St Paul's Bay, and Peter, without taking his eyes off the road, indicated the small island on which the saint was said to have landed.

'According to legend—and to historians—St Paul spent some time here,' he told her. 'He converted the Roman governor of the island, and for a while settled down in a small villa, just up there in the hills.' He pointed to some rocky ground just above the little town. 'The villa has recently been excavated, and early Christian symbols have been found, proving that St Paul probably did live there.' He smiled slightly. 'Not that the people of the villages need that sort of proof. They have always known.'

The road began to climb, winding steeply through sandy hills strewn with umbrella pines, and then it descended again to another wide bay, the Bay of Mellieha. Here the beach was long and golden, littered with sun umbrellas, and the spot was obviously a tourists' paradise. There was a village of Mellieha, neat and well ordered like most of the villages Catriona had seen, but it clung to the southern arm of the bay, and beyond, save for a solitary modern luxury hotel, there were few buildings.

'Once,' the Count told her, as they cruised along a

low-lying road that ran beside the beach, 'the Turkish fleet attempted to make a landing here, but they were defeated. There was a massacre, and it's said that the waters of the bay ran crimson with their blood.'

Catriona shivered. 'How horrible!'

He looked faintly amused. 'People should learn not to trouble their neighbours.'

'But was it necessary to resist the invaders with quite so much brutality?'

'If one had no wish to be massacred oneself—yes. No doubt it was necessary.'

She turned her head to look at him. In another age he, too, could have been cruel and ruthless. It was all there, in the strong, aggressive jaw, the narrow mouth, the aquiline nose. She realised now that it was one of the things, that night at the Calverley Hotel, which she had sensed about him. He was descended from mediaeval warlords—harsh, merciless men whose sunbaked island had been a constant battleground—and it showed clearly in his face. She wondered what it might have been like to be at the mercy of a sixteenth-century Count Vilhena, and involuntarily she shivered again.

Beyond Mellieha they climbed another hill, the road twisting alarmingly past dry fields, a few carob trees and a second lonely fortress. It took them some time to reach the summit, but when they did an amazing panorama lay spread in front of them.

Below was the gently rounded tip of the island, and the tiny harbour of Marsa. There was a small landing-stage and one or two buildings, but otherwise the rocky shoreline had not been scarred by man, and it had an unspoilt, almost primitive look. The

encircling sea was the colour of amethyst, deep and
vivid, a shock to the senses. Catriona leant forward,
gazing through the windscreen. Beyond the sparkling
water, following the line of the horizon, there was a
hazy, rose-coloured blur that looked almost like
another island. She stared, fascinated.

'That shape over there—it's like a mirage,' she
said a little breathlessly.

Peter spared the distant blur a momentary glance.
'That's Gozo,' he told her briefly.

'It's beautiful.'

He said nothing. Slowly they descended the hill,
and in a rough car park near the landing-stage they
stopped. Rather violently, he jerked the handbrake
into position.

'We'll leave the car here,' he said. 'It will be safe
enough, and my boat is not far away.' He climbed
out, Catriona following his example, and they started
walking towards the shore. A white steamer was just
pulling away from the landing-stage, and he explained that she formed part of the Government-run
ferry service.

'There are several steamers,' he told her, 'all of
them equipped to carry cars and lorries as well as foot
passengers. For them, the crossing takes a little less
than half an hour, but it won't take us quite as long
as that.'

She followed him across the road that led down to
the landing-stage. Already one or two cars had begun
to queue, waiting for the next ferry, and she wondered how their occupants were going to stand the
heat. Stumbling after Peter, she gazed across the
water at the haunting, beckoning outline of Malta's
sister island, and a line from Keats began to run

through her head. *Faery lands forlorn.* . . .

Near the water's edge, about a hundred yards from the road, there was a smart, white-painted boathouse and close to it a private jetty had been constructed. Both, it seemed, belonged to the Vilhena family. Alongside the jetty a graceful white launch lay rocking on the morning tide, and as they walked towards her a small boy who had been sitting cross-legged in the shadow of the boathouse scrambled to his feet. Running to catch up with them, he said something in Maltese, and the Count placed a hand in his trouser pocket. There was a glint of sunlight on silver, and the boy smiled widely, revealing flawless teeth.

'*Grazzi, signur.*' Clutching his booty, he backed slowly away, as if withdrawing from the presence of royalty, then he turned and scuttled out of sight round a corner of the boathouse.

'Who was that?' Catriona asked, amused.

'The grandson of my boatman. This launch, *Sultana*, has been afloat for half an hour. He has been watching to make sure that she could not be stolen.'

'Was there a chance that she might have been?' Catriona asked.

'Not the slightest possibility. We have some extremely sophisticated security devices, and the most experienced thief would be unwise to tamper with them. But Joseph must not be deprived of employment. One day, with encouragement, he will turn into a fine boatman. Or, at least, he will become a useful worker in my shipyard.'

He placed a hand beneath her elbow, and she stepped into the launch. As she sat down she discovered that the seats were surprisingly comfortable, and she noticed, too, that the craft had evidently been equipped with very little thought for expense.

Lightly, Peter swung himself down beside her, and with a roar the engine came to life. He swung the wheel and they moved forward, curving away from the jetty. White foam sparkled behind them and they plunged a little, becoming entangled in the wake of the ferry steamer. Catriona felt a sharp thrill of excitement.

'You are a good sailor?' he wanted to know. She saw that he was smiling slightly.

'I'm not likely to be seasick, if that's what you mean. My father took me sailing quite a lot.'

'Excellent,' he smiled dryly. 'I shan't have to put you ashore.'

Gathering speed, they headed out to sea. Malta—and the slower moving ferry steamer—had fallen away behind them, and the world consisted of sea and sky. Spray hung in the air, as they seemed to bound over the sparkling water. Peter handled the launch with casual confidence, and Catriona realised that he was probably as much at home in a boat as he was on dry land. After a time, partly to break the silence between them, she asked a question.

'How long have your family been building boats?'

'My father started the business, after the last war. We had lost a lot of money, and it was a time when if one wished to survive one had to be practical. Fortunately, my father was a practical man. Fishermen on his Gozo estates had been building their own boats for centuries, but left to themselves they would never have been able to develop their skill into a commercial asset. My father had the imagination and the business sense to turn the thing into a thriving

industry. After a time he brought in additional work-
men, young, specially trained boatbuilders. We
started to produce small yachts, and a few years later
began developing motor cruisers, too. Soon we were
selling all over the world. At the moment we concentrate mainly on cabin cruisers and racing yachts.'

'It all sounds very interesting,' Catriona said.
'Quite a responsibility, though.'

'It means a lot of work, yes. I need to keep a fairly
close eye on things.'

'You must work very hard.'

She saw his hands tighten on the wheel. 'What else
is there? Life without work is pointless.'

She opened her mouth to say something, to protest aloud that he was wrong, but then she remembered the things he had said the night before, and
checked herself in time. Peter did not make any effort
to expand his views.

Gozo was much closer now, and she could see that
it was an island of high, rocky cliffs. There seemed to
be more vegetation than she had noticed in Malta
and there were even woods running down to the
beach. In fact, it was the most romantic-looking
place she had ever seen. They were moving in quite
rapidly, and it wasn't long before the cliffs were
looming above them. Over to their right a large village climbed the slopes behind a fairly modern-
looking harbour, and she could see that the ferryboat
was headed that way, but they had a different destination. They turned westwards, along the coast, and
as they did so their speed dropped.

A stone's throw away, on the starboard side, a
majestic, glistening cliff-face reared itself against the
sky. At the foot of the cliff, piles of jagged rock were

scattered, as if thrown down by the hand of a playful giant, and once or twice they passed great openings in the granite wall—black, mysterious caverns that would have done credit to far-fetched tales of smuggling and piracy. Just here, so close to the shore, the sea was as calm as an inland lake, and as translucent as glass. Gazing down into the depths, Catriona found that fish and drifting fronds of seaweed were clearly visible a very long way below the surface. She thought what a wonderful spot it would be for underwater swimming.

Aloud, she said: 'There must be a lot of diving around here. The conditions are perfect, aren't they?'

Peter didn't answer, and for a moment she thought he hadn't heard what she said. She was about to repeat the question when he spoke, and to her astonishment his voice was sharp with anger.

'Maria! Must you ask so many questions? This is not a radio interview, and I am not a representative of the Tourist Board. I should not have brought you with me—I thought you knew how to be quiet.'

His voice echoed against the cliffs, and mockingly the sound was thrown back. Catriona stared at him, shaken and bewildered.

'I'm sorry,' she said quietly

For several minutes there was no sound but the steady chugging of the engine. Peter was staring straight in front of him, and he was frowning. She realised that, suddenly, he was in a very tense mood, and she wondered why. Was it because they had reached Gozo? Was there, perhaps, something in the strange, wild place that haunted him? Why *had* he brought her with him? Because, for some reason, he hadn't wanted to come alone?

They rounded a corner and suddenly the cliffs fell away, giving place to a long sandy beach, backed by untidy dunes. At the far end of the beach there was a cluster of iron-roofed, workmanlike modern buildings, and as they drew nearer Catriona saw that there was also a landing-stage. They turned inwards, slipping smoothly alongside a tall jetty, and a man appeared above them, stripped to the waist. At sight of Peter he smiled, and they exchanged greetings in Maltese. Between them they made the boat secure, and with the agility of long practice Peter sprang ashore.

Catriona stood up, and ignoring the hands held out to her made a determined effort to disembark without assistance. She was not successful. The toe of her right sandal caught beneath the gunwale and she tripped, very nearly precipitating herself into the water. For a moment she wobbled precariously, in imminent danger of falling overboard, and the boat rocked beneath her as she struggled to regain her balance. Then hard brown hands—Peter Vilhena's hands—caught her by the waist and lifted her bodily on to the landing-stage.

'You should have told me you had no recent experience of boats. It is an advantage to be aware of such things.'

His voice was sharp with sudden anger, and his hands were not gentle as he set her on her feet.

She looked up at him, startled by the fury in his face. For a moment she was too taken aback to respond, then she felt anger taking possession of her.

'I can swim,' she retorted crisply. 'If you'd prefer it, though, I'll go back to Malta by ferry.'

He stared at her, then turned impatiently away. 'I

shall be extremely busy this morning, and I shan't
have much time to spare. You had better have a look
at the village of Mixija, which is not far from here. If
you come to the office, someone will give you a lift.'

She opened her mouth to protest, but had no
opportunity to say anything, for he immediately
strode away along the jetty. The other man, who had
been watching her with an air of puzzled apprecia-
tion, fell in beside him, and she could do nothing but
follow them, for the heat was tremendous and there
was no possibility of lingering by the unshaded water-
front.

The 'office' turned out to be a square hut with a
roof of corrugated iron and a single window that
badly needed cleaning. Inside, there was a deal table
littered with diagrams and typewritten lists, and the
walls were covered by giant photographs of yachts
and motorboats. Two men were bent over a chart
that had been spread out at one end of the table, but
because of a radio playing noisily in one corner of the
room they didn't hear their employer's approach
until his shadow fell across them. The older of the two
became aware of his presence first.

'*Bon giorn, signur.*' Straightening hurriedly, he
nudged his companion, who went over to turn the
radio off. Then they all began talking in Maltese.

Half wishing she had not come, Catriona seated
herself on a hard wooden stool and waited while they
discussed, at considerable length, whatever it was the
charts represented. She felt out of place, even slightly
ridiculous, and she was embarrassed by the interested
stares of the men. A large fan, mounted on the ceiling, rendered the temperature in the hut reasonably
bearable, but she knew that outside it was like an

inferno, and she couldn't imagine what she was going to do.

At last the discussion came to some sort of conclusion, and belatedly Peter remembered her. He turned and walked over to her, but she could see that irritation was still strong in his face.

'I am going on a tour of inspection,' he told her. 'I shall be busy for two hours, maybe more. One of the men will drive you to the village, where you will be able to obtain a cool drink.'

She stood up, eyeing him in disbelief. 'A cool drink won't keep me occupied for two hours, and it's too hot to walk about much. Couldn't I go round with you? I'd much rather see the boatyard.'

He sighed, rather as if his patience were about to give out. 'Perhaps, but I have important work to do, and I shall much prefer it if you wait for me in Mixija. Besides, if you don't wish to walk about in the heat I would not advise you to linger here.' His expression grew a little less hostile. 'The church contains a particularly fine painting, said to be the work of Caravaggio. I am sure you will find it interesting.' Without waiting for a reply, he turned to one of the men. 'Joe, drive this lady to the village. Put her down in the *piazza*, them come back here.'

For the second time that morning Catriona opened her mouth to protest, but no sound emerged. Grinning from ear to ear, Joe produced a bunch of keys from his pocket, and she found herself being escorted outside. On the shady side of the building a battered little Triumph had been parked, and with elaborate courtesy the Maltese held a door open for her.

She got in, and when he had succeeded in closing the door, which appeared to possess a faulty lock, he climbed in beside her. At the fourth or fifth attempt he managed to get the engine going, and this success appeared to afford him considerable satisfaction.

'Today,' he remarked, 'I am lucky.'

They swung round in a circle, and clouds of acrid smoke from the exhaust pipe found their way in through Catriona's window. A selection of dolls, dangling from the windscreen, danced grotesquely as they roared away up a narrow, bumpy track. At the first bend they narrowly missed an oncoming donkey cart, and Catriona, closing her eyes, hoped Joe's luck was destined to hold.

The Maltese was clearly curious about her, but he was also discreet and in his way the soul of courtesy. When they reached the village, a small collection of houses gathered round a wide square and an imposing church, he set her down beside the café and recommended her, with avuncular solicitude, to keep out of the sun.

'In there, they look after you.' He grinned more widely than ever. 'Enjoy yourself, lady!'

He was gone, roaring away across the square in a cloud of dust, and Catriona was left standing alone on the pavement, feeling very much as if she had just been deposited in the midst of the Sahara.

At first she didn't feel particularly inclined to go into the café, partly because it had been Peter's suggestion that she should do so and partly because, if external appearances were anything to go by, the place wasn't exactly tempting. As far as she could see, the dust of several summers had been allowed to settle undisturbed on the narrow window ledges, the faded paintwork was peeling everywhere and the doorway was covered by a decidedly grubby curtain of beads. But it was too hot to stand about in the open for long, and when eventually she plucked up enough courage to push the curtain aside, she found that behind it things were slightly more reassuring. There were three or four formica-topped tables, all of them spotlessly clean, and the tiled floor was bright and well polished. One wall was dominated by a painting of the Virgin Mary, another by a faded photograph of what appeared to be a local football team, and on a third someone had hung a picture of the Queen, evidently cut from a magazine and lovingly framed. Beneath all three pictures there were small bunches of flowers.

From somewhere at the back of the place a plump young woman appeared carrying a tray of glasses. She was wearing a shabby black dress and one of her front teeth was missing, but she had an endearingly cheerful smile, and she didn't seem particularly taken aback by the sight of Catriona.

'It's hot, my goodness!' Picking up a newspaper, she fanned herself vigorously. 'You like something cool, *signurina*?'

'Yes, please.' Catriona sat down, taking off her sunglasses, and the other woman studied her with increased interest.

'You tourist?' she enquired, pouring something brown and fizzy into a tumbler.

'Not exactly. I have a job—in Malta.'

'But you're on holiday today, uh?'

'Yes.' She got up and went to collect her drink from the counter. 'What is it?' she asked curiously. 'It's not Coca-Cola.'

'No, no, it's what we call Kinnie. It's good for you, there are herbs in it.'

Catriona tasted the sparkling drink. It was slightly bitter, but ice-cold and very refreshing. 'I like it,' she said. 'It's just right, somehow.'

The girl started polishing glasses. 'You like Malta, lady?'

'Very much.'

'I don't like Malta.' She gestured expressively. 'Everywhere hotels and restaurants, and people running about.'

'You have tourists here, too, don't you?'

'Not many—not in Mixija. We don't need to make money that way. All the boys work for *is-Signur* . . . always plenty of jobs in his boatyard.'

Catriona felt herself stiffen slightly. 'The men get well paid, then?'

The girl nodded. 'They get a lot of money. And Count Vilhena is so nice—my goodness, he is a kind man!'

'He is?'

'Just like a brother to the young ones, and a son to the old men. Always he worries about the village. He would do anything for any of us.'

Slightly taken aback, Catriona digested this information. 'Everybody likes him, then?'

'I tell you. . . .' The Gozitan girl spread her hands expressively. 'I love him like he was my uncle.'

Catriona stared hard into her glass. She couldn't think of an appropriate reply, and though dozens of questions flew into her mind she somehow couldn't bring herself to ask any of them. She longed to keep the conversation going, to find out more, but suddenly, unaccountably, she felt selfconscious. She said nothing further, and the girl behind the bar, turning on a radio, filled the room with the voice of Elvis Presley.

'*I'm not made of wood, and I don't have a wooden heart. . . .*'

Catriona stood up abruptly and paid for her Kinnie. The Gozitan girl looked surprised.

'You got your own car out there, lady?'

'No, someone is coming to collect me—in about an hour, I think. I'd just like to go and have a look at your church.'

She slipped out, through the whispering curtain of beads, into fierce sunlight and walked across the *pjazza* to the church. Its massive honey-coloured façade soared above her, and as she climbed the steps an unseen bell began chiming the hour. It was eleven o'clock.

Inside, the air was cool and heavy with incense. By comparison with an English country church, the basilica seemed vast, but its vastness was oddly soothing. There was something reassuring about the candles glimmering on the altar and before the figures of the saints, and a deep and timeless peace hung in the atmosphere. It was a peace almost as real and inescapable as the overpowering scent of incense. Beside one of the great pillars an old priest was kneeling alone, lost in prayer or silent meditation, and his tranquil stillness was so impressive that Catriona, for a moment, couldn't resist stopping to stare.

Such peaceful detachment, of course, was part of the religious life. It wasn't really within the reach of ordinary people in the everyday world. But, even so, there was such a thing as being at peace with oneself, even when one was caught up in the rough-and-tumble of normal human existence. Anyone could possess inner tranquillity. Until a few days ago Catriona had felt that she possessed it herself.

So what had happened?

She moved closer to the High Altar, and stood gazing upwards at the wonderful painting that formed the reredos. Jesus and the Children. . . . It was an unusually gentle subject for the dramatic hand of Caravaggio, but though she was no expert on the Masters she could see that it might well have been his work. Human beings could be surprising, sometimes.

Slowly she turned away from the altar, and as she wandered back down the long aisle she found herself wondering whether it could be true that Peter Vilhena was capable of so much kindness and humanity. She supposed it must be true, at least as far as his own people were concerned, for the girl in the café was not likely to have been making things up as she went along. Helpless, dependent people obviously brought out the best in him, and that didn't surprise her, for almost from the beginning she had realised that his strength was not the strength of cruelty. At least, he would never be cruel to those not in a position to hit back.

Once again she emerged into the sunshine, and as she stood hesitating on the church steps it struck her that sooner or later, probably within the next week or two, she would be going back to England. She would be leaving Peter Vilhena behind her, together with all the complexities of his enigmatic nature, and she wouldn't need to think about him any more. This Maltese episode would be a closed chapter in her life. It would belong to the past. She would just have to turn the page and go on to something else.

Waves of depression rolled over her, and she stared

unseeingly at a nearby oleander. Then her ears caught the sound of an approaching car, and seconds later the vehicle came into view. It was bumping its way round the square, a cloud of dust rising behind it, and she recognised the ancient Triumph in which she had been driven from the boatyard. With a protesting squeal of brakes the car slid to a halt in front of her, and the driver got out.

Catriona stared. It wasn't the workman who had brought her up from the shore. It was Peter Vilhena himself.

Slowly she descended the steps. As she drew nearer to him she could see that he looked rather tired, and there was something in his face she didn't understand.

'Get in,' he advised, 'before you are overtaken by sunstroke.'

Remembering his attitude earlier in the day, she hesitated. Stiffly, she said: 'I'm perfectly all right, really. If you're still busy. . . .'

'I'm not.'

Rather reluctantly she settled herself in the front passenger seat, and he got in beside her.

'You have seen something of Mixija?' he wanted to know.

'Not really, it's been too hot to walk around. But the church is wonderful, and that painting. . . .' She gestured expressively. 'The villagers must be very proud of it.'

'They are. There has been some disagreement about the identity of the artist, but most experts attribute it to Caravaggio. He did, after all, spend quite a lot of time in the Maltese islands, and several of his works are known to have been left here.'

'I'm not surprised that he wanted to come here. There's so much to paint. Gozo, particularly. One day I'd like to come back with my colours and brushes.'

'Gozo has many facets,' he told her. 'Not all of them can be represented on canvas.'

He started the engine, and they drove slowly round the square before turning into a narrow alley-way which, after a time, widened into a lane. As they passed, chickens scattered and children flattened themselves against the drystone walls. Dust clouds hung in the air behind them, and the heat was intense.

Catriona felt she had to say something. 'Are we going back to Malta now?'

'Not yet.' Peter guided the car carefully round a narrow bend. 'We shall, I hope, be back in time for lunch, but I have one more task to complete.'

'Oh! I thought you said. . . .'

'This has nothing to do with business.'

The road rose steeply, leaving the village behind. On one side, cultivated terraces sloped gently to-wards the sea. On the other, more terraces climbed the rocky hillside above them. Every so often, a carob tree bent its gnarled shape across the roadway, and grotesque clumps of prickly pear huddled behind the low stone walls. It was greener, more beautiful and more primitive than Malta.

They travelled for about a mile, twisting their way upwards through the rocky countryside, always with-in sight of the sea, and then they came to a pair of gates—tall iron gates mounted on massive stone piers. The gates were standing wide, and beyond them a dusty track wound out of sight through a grove of pine trees.

They slowed and turned in through the gateway, lurching violently over the uneven, neglected track. Catriona stared at the strange, exotic jumble of growth hemming them in on either side, and was reminded suddenly of some child's picture-book version of a lost, idyllic South Sea island. Hibiscus, oleander and rose bushes jostled one another among the pine trees, and there were other flowers, too, that she could not identify. Through a gap in the trees on one side of the road she glimpsed the beginnings of an olive grove and also the remains of a path, now choked by overgrown bushes, that had once led towards it.

She glanced at the man beside her. So far he had said nothing and offered no explanations. He seemed more taut and withdrawn than ever. Somehow, Catriona couldn't bring herself to ask questions. Besides, the rasping, noisy engine made conversation almost an impossibility.

They rounded a sharp bend, emerged abruptly from the little wood and there, in front of them, was a house. It was built of stone, mellow, golden stone that had witnessed many centuries of sunlight, and in shape it resembled a small French château. At one end of the building there was a circular tower, windows were scattered erratically about its massive walls, and in front there was a wide terrace. Trees and shrubs had been allowed to run riot all around, and in its isolation, half abandoned by man, the place had acquired a lost and secret look.

Peter switched off the engine and without a word he got out of the car. Catriona followed his example and the warm stillness came at her as if it were a living thing. She looked at Peter.

'Where are we?'

He didn't answer at once. Instead he stood looking around him, his gaze travelling slowly over the old walls, the rutted driveway, the wild, deserted remains of what had once been a garden.

'It's my family home,' he said at last. 'Or it was. Chajn Lucia . . . the Fountain of Lucia.'

'It's so beautiful,' Catriona said slowly. 'I've never seen anything like it.'

She looked up at the front of the house. Quite a long way up, there was a window that opened on to a small rounded balcony, a balcony that might have been designed for the use of Romeo and Juliet. She thought of Peter's ancestors, those mysterious, vaguely exciting people who had once lived in this house, and wondered if their colourful ghosts ever wandered in the tangled gardens or lingered on the little balcony. From that height, she thought, it must be possible to look out across the tops of the pine trees to the waters of the nearby Mediterranean.

From one of his pockets Peter had produced a large, ornate brass key, and was inserting it in the lock of the front door. Rather reluctantly it turned, and the door swung inwards. Fascinated, but half feeling that she was a trespasser, Catriona remained where she was.

'If you're going to have a look round I'll wait for you here,' she said uncertainly.

'Why?' he demanded, inspecting the door's rusty hinges with a critical eye.

'Well. . . .' She shrugged helplessly, not knowing quite what to say.

Suddenly he looked round at her. 'Come inside,'

he said. 'You'll be perfectly safe. I did not bring you here with seduction in mind.'

A flush spread beneath her tan. 'I only meant. . . .' she began.

'Well, whatever you meant, would you be good enough to come inside? I'm here to look at my house, and it will be annoying if I have to keep remembering that I've left you on the doorstep. Of course, if you would really prefer not to see the house, perhaps you would like to wait in the car.'

'Oh, no, I'd like to see it—very much,' she said meekly, running up the steps.

He stood aside, allowing her to precede him into a large square room dominated by a graceful wooden staircase. At one time, probably, the stairs had been polished, carefully and regularly, but some time had elapsed since any kind of care had been lavished on them, and the shallow treads were coated with fine yellow dust. Cobwebs clung between the banisters and a dead butterfly lay where it had last fluttered, on the bottom stair.

Catriona looked around her. The floorboards were dusty, too, and the windows were very dirty. Apart from a telephone, which had been left on the floor, there did not appear to be any furniture in the place. She glanced at Peter in bewilderment.

'Why is it empty?'

At some time a piece of plaster had fallen from the ceiling and now it lay in a hundred fragments on the floor near the foot of the stairs. Peter bent to examine it. Evenly, he said:

'A few years ago I had the furniture removed and the place locked up.'

'But why?'

Frowning, he pushed a door open and walked through into another room. Catriona followed, and gasped at the sight of a magnificent plaster ceiling. She gazed up at it.

'What do the figures represent?'

He answered without glancing at the ceiling. 'The figure on the left, playing a harp, is meant to be King David. His music is driving an evil spirit from the heart of Saul.' He threw the scene a cursory glance. 'I suppose it needs restoration pretty badly.'

Catriona stood in the doorway, watching him as he casually tested a rotting floorboard with his foot. 'This is a wonderful place,' she said. 'Why did you stop using it?'

He shrugged. 'I had a reason. While we're here we had better look at the rest of the house, but I don't want to waste too much time.' His voice was clipped and unemotional, but at the same time Catriona sensed that he was in a very unusual mood.

Talking less and less, they toured the rest of the ground floor, and her heart warmed to the charm of the old house. There was a sort of morning-room, originally intended for the ladies of the family, and also a small library equipped with French windows that had once opened into a tiny courtyard. Now, the library's walls were lined with empty shelves, and coarse yellow grass pushed its way between the flagstones in the courtyard. The old *salotto*, once the heart of the house, now brooded in silence behind shuttered windows, and its doors had been attacked by woodworm. Alcoves which had once accommodated rare porcelain now harboured nothing but cobwebs, and winter rains, beating hard against the eastern wall, had caused widespread patches of damp.

'Did your parents live here?' Catriona asked, still shocked by the abandonment of so much that was beautiful and that had once been cherished.

'For much of the time, yes. My mother preferred it to Malta.'

'Then you must have grown up here.'

'Yes.'

She found herself visualising Peter as a child, an incredibly good-looking and probably quite adorable small boy, and she watched him as he threw open one of the windows. Pushing the shutters back, he stared out into the garden, and she thought that he looked curiously young now, young and vulnerable, as if this visit to his old home had somehow stripped him of his defences—the hard veneer that normally made it difficult to get close to him. She wondered whether Jacqueline had ever been to Ghajn Lucia—and then, resolutely, she pushed Jacqueline out of her mind.

Peter was staring fixedly at the sky. 'There's a cloud,' he said.

She moved across the room and looked over his shoulder. A cloud, small but very dark, had appeared over the pine trees and was drifting slowly westwards.

'It's so small,' she objected.

'M'mm.' He glanced at his watch. 'I shall check the rest of the house, and then we had better be going.'

He fastened the faded shutters, sliding a large bolt firmly into place, and as he did so Catriona wondered rather sadly how much time would elapse before they were opened again.

They went through into the kitchen, which was large, Victorian in design and in need of extensive removation. The antiquated sink was the size of a horse trough, and a blackened stove that had once been used for cooking might easily have been on display in a museum. Above one of the doors there was a large, silent clock. Its hands stopped at a quarter to nine.

At last, after a cursory inspection of various sculleries and pantries, they went back to the hall and began to climb the main staircase. Peter was very silent now, and all around them the brooding, throbbing stillness seemed to have deepened. Catriona felt an almost unbearable tension beginning to take possession of her.

The staircase rose gradually, curling round on itself, and foolishly Catriona started counting the stairs. There were twenty-five of them. She reached the top ahead of Peter, who had paused to examine some telltale traces of woodworm and for a moment she leant against the balustrade at the top, looking down on his dark head. As she did so something stirred inside her—something she didn't understand. . . .

And then she heard the thunder.

At first it was little more than a murmur, gentle and distant, but seconds later it came again and this time it was an ominous growl, drawing steadily nearer. Peter abandoned the woodworm and swiftly covered the remaining stairs.

'That's close,' he said lightly. 'I'll take a look and see what's going on out there.'

He passed through an archway, crossed a wide landing, and opened a door that was directly opposite the head of the stairs. Catriona waited a moment, then rather hesitantly she followed him, realising as she crossed the threshold that it was the room with the Romeo and Juliet balcony. Peter was already unfastening the long windows that opened on to the balcony, and as she glanced past him she saw that she had been right to imagine the room would have a wonderful view. Beyond the tree-tops she could see the magnificent curve of the Mediterranean, and she realised at once that it would be a superb vantage point from which to watch a summer sunrise.

Then she looked again, and saw that the sea was an ominous mauvish grey. A line of cloud had built up along the horizon and as she watched there was a vivid flash of forked lightning, followed almost immediately by a slightly louder rumble of thunder.

Catriona shrank back, fighting to control her own reactions, ashamed of the shudders running through her. She hated thunder—how she hated it! Peter was out on the balcony, staring out to sea, but she didn't join him, and it wasn't until she heard the soft whisper of water falling on dry ground that she realised it was raining.

In Malta, she knew, there was never any rain between May and the end of August. During those weeks the islands just roasted beneath the ruthless sun. But now it had come, and the dry, dusty days were over. The rain went on falling, lightly and very softly, almost like dew, and when she drew near to the open window Catriona could feel the gentle touch of moisture on her face. For the first time in her life she appreciated how very much like a miracle a shower of rain could seem.

Then another shaft of lightning flickered in front of them, and this time the thunder was much louder. Catriona tensed, her fingernails digging into the palms of her hands. Whatever happened, Peter Vilhena must not be allowed to guess how much she hated the storm. Making a supreme effort, she steeled herself and went out to join him on the balcony.

He turned his head slowly and their eyes met. A tremor ran through Catriona, and she knew it had nothing to do with her fear of the storm, but when she tried to look away from him she couldn't. His dark gaze was holding hers and she didn't even want to break away.

Thunder rolled directly overhead. It seemed to shake the house, and from the tops of the pine-trees a flock of birds rose in panic. Catriona drew back against the window-frame, shattered by emotions that were tearing her in two. He wouldn't understand . . . nobody could.

'What's the matter?' he asked. His voice was taut. 'You're not afraid of thunder?'

She shook her head desperately. 'It's something that happened a long time ago.' To her horror, a tear hovered on the end of her lashes.

'What happened?' He moved closer to her, and she could feel his breath on her cheek. His nearness made her slightly dizzy.

'My parents quarrelled—during a thunderstorm.' She didn't add that she could hear their voices still— her father's bitterly angry, her mother's hard and defensive.

There was a tiny silence. When Peter spoke his voice was very gentle. 'Does it matter . . . now?'

'I suppose not. But my mother left after that quarrel. She never came back.'

Almost before she knew what was happening, his arms were round her and he was holding her so

tightly that she could scarcely breathe. Pulses
throbbed wildly all over her body and she gasped,
clinging to him, overwhelmed by the sudden realisation that this was where she had wanted to be.
Dazedly, she wondered whether there had ever been
a time when she had not longed to be in his arms.
Then rational thought became an impossibility, for
his lips were on hers and the pine-tops swayed
erratically. As the kiss went on the whole world
lurched, and she knew that for her nothing would
ever be the same again.

At last he released her mouth and pressed his
cheek, damp with rain, against hers. Thunder
rumbled again, but this time it was a little farther
away, and in any case she hardly heard it. Nothing
was real any more, nothing in the world mattered,
except Peter—the strength of his arms about her, the
feel of his lips, the way his eyelashes fluttered against
her cheek. Her fingers entwined themselves in his
hair, and as he kissed her again she felt that she was
drowning in ecstasy.

Somewhere, a telephone was ringing. Catriona
didn't recognise the sound at first, and anyway it
didn't seem to matter. But the shrilling was very per-
sistent, and after a time Peter lifted his head. His hold
relaxed a little, and she sensed that he was drawing
away from her. Her arms about his neck, she willed
him to come back, but already the spell was broken.
He looked down into her face, his eyes unreadable,
and she felt a stab of uneasiness. How could he look
at her like that? It was as if—almost as if he were
trying to remember who she was.

Gently he released her. 'I must answer the telephone,' he said. 'No one would contact me here if it

were not important.'

He stepped through the window into the empty room beyond, and she heard his footsteps echoing firmly along the passageway and down the stairs.

CHAPTER TEN

It had stopped raining and the clouds were moving on, drifting across the island. Catriona stood where Peter had left her, one hand resting on the iron balustrade. She wondered why it was that she didn't seem to be able to move. Perhaps, she thought, it was because she had taken a step into the unknown, and the ground seemed to have crumbled away beneath her feet.

Very slowly she took a firm grip on herself. She heard the telephone stop ringing, but the walls of the old house were very thick, and she couldn't hear Peter's voice. Eventually she wandered inside, and had just reached the head of the stairs when he appeared below her. He didn't look up, and when he spoke his voice sounded odd.

'That was Antoinette. She wanted to remind me that we all have an engagement this evening.'

'An engagement?' Catriona repeated.

'A theatrical presentation in the gardens of Castel Verdala, our Governor's country residence.' There was a pause, then he went on, 'It's a performance of *Twelfth Night*. Jacqueline has the part of Olivia.'

Catriona's fingers curled tightly around the balustrade.

'In any case,' Peter went on, 'it is time we were going. The storm is moving on and there will be no more rain for several hours, but it may return later. We should get back to Malta as quickly as possible.'

For several seconds Catriona stood still. She didn't understand. Had she dreamt those moments on the balcony? Was it only in her imagination that a few minutes earlier. . . .

Feeling like a sleepwalker, she moved down the stairs. They left the house by the front door and Peter locked it behind them, turning the heavy brass key. Outside, it was still very warm, but the air was much fresher and there was no longer an all-pervading smell of dust. The leaves were a brighter green. The old, battered Triumph actually looked cleaner. But Catriona hardly noticed. She just got into the car and sat staring in front of her.

Peter drove very fast, almost recklessly, and as they made their way down the drive, through the jungle of newly washed growth, she tried to guess at the thoughts that might be passing through his head. But his face remained set, impassive, and he didn't speak until they reached the gates. Then he glanced round.

'I'm sorry,' he said abruptly.

Catriona moistened her dry lips. 'What—what for?'

'I think you understand what I mean.' His voice grated a little. 'I don't usually behave in that sort of way. Please forget it.'

Forget it!

She stared hard through the newly washed windscreen, willing the tears to stay away. Could he really be so insensitive? Hadn't he recognised her response at all? Didn't he realise she was in love with him?

The words echoed through her head almost as if she had spoken them aloud. She, who in all her adult life had never felt more than mildly attracted to any man, was now in love herself—so much in love that the pain was almost more than she could bear.

She couldn't trust her voice, so she didn't say anything, and after a minute or two he spoke again.

'When we first met, Catriona,' he said very quietly, 'you made your feelings clear. You once called me a parasite, and you may have been right. There was a time, I believe, when I was a little different, but that ended twelve years ago.'

She looked at him. 'What happened—twelve years ago?'

He shrugged. 'You must have wondered why Ghajn Lucia was abandoned.'

'Yes, I suppose I did.'

'Well, as I told you, it was our family home. Most Maltese families don't spend too much time over here on Gozo, but my parents were particularly fond of the place, and anyway, my father had his boatyard here. When I was a boy I spent more time at Ghajn Lucia than anywhere else in the Islands. I loved it. I didn't want to live anywhere else.' He paused, and she noticed that his knuckles were white, as his hands gripped the steering-wheel. 'My father had a brother, Tomas. They were partners in the family business, so, naturally, Uncle Tomas also spent much of his time on Gozo, and when he came to see us he brought his daughter, Marina.' The strong voice hesitated and then went on. 'I taught Marina to sail, and together we explored every nook and corner of the Gozo coast. When I was twenty-two years old and she was eighteen we became engaged to be married, but my uncle would not allow her to go through with the wedding until she reached her nineteenth birthday. He said no girl should be married so young, that she needed more time.'

'What—what happened?' Catriona asked.

He stared hard at the twisting road in front of them. 'She was a strong swimmer, and she loved sailing. One spring afternoon she took a small racing yacht out into the bay. While she was out the Sirocco sprang up . . . the warm wind from Africa. Because she was alone she could not cope. The yacht was smashed against a small island off the coast of Malta—they call it Filfla, it's a sanctuary for birds. When they found her, a day or so later, her father could not identify her, but I knew her by the ring she was wearing. I had given it to her.'

Catriona closed her eyes, trying to shut out the horror of it. 'I'm sorry,' she said, and knew that no words had ever sounded more inadequate. She wanted to throw her arms around him—somehow, to find a way of putting an end to his suffering. But she couldn't, because he didn't want her.

All at once everything fell into place. His embittered outlook on life, his feeling that at times it was hardly worth living—everything made sense now. And she thought, miserably, that she even knew why he had kissed her back there on the balcony. In that moment he had just needed somebody. That was all.

They were passing through Mixija now, and within a few minutes they would be at the boatyard.

'I did not intend to tell you about Marina,' he said suddenly, 'and I did not mention her because I wanted your sympathy, but because I wished you to understand that I shall never fall in love again. I shall marry, but that is another matter. My wife will be an intelligent woman with her own interests, sensible in her approach to marriage. She will appreciate the position I can give her, but she will never expect me to pretend that I am in love with her. I would not marry on any other terms.'

Staring blindly ahead, Catriona wondered if he considered that Jacqueline Calleja would meet his requirements in this respect. Probably he did. After all, he was hurrying back to Malta because he didn't want to miss her interpretation of Olivia. On the other hand, why, until Toni telephoned, had he apparently forgotten all about the performance? Why had he chosen that day, of all days, for a visit to Gozo?

They jolted down on to the quayside, and Catriona forced herself to speak.

'Don't you think there's a—a possibility? Don't you think you might one day meet someone who could change your mind?'

The car came to a halt, and he switched the engine off. 'It's too late.'

The *Sultana* was waiting for them, bobbing gently on the water, and without speaking again he handed Catriona aboard. All the clouds had moved over now, and the sky was once again a tranquil blue. In the clear, strong light of early afternoon they swung away from the jetty and headed back towards Malta.

During the short return trip they hardly talked at all, and that at least was a relief to Catriona, for she could not possibly have maintained a normal conversation. Being so close to Peter was wonderful or, at least, it could have been. But she knew that in every important sense he was as far away from her as it was possible to be, and because of that her whole body ached. She thought of Marina, the girl who had died, and wondered what she had been like. They had both been so young. Could they really have been so deeply, so completely in love that there could never be anything else for the one who was left behind?

Then she pulled herself up short and forced herself to face the fact that, probably, in the end, there would be someone else for Peter. He just had to meet the right girl. Although he might not realise it yet, it was possible that he had already met her in the person of Jacqueline. Catriona herself was not the right one, and perhaps, in the kindest way possible, he had been trying to tell her that. Obviously, he had moments of intense, agonising depression—even despair—and in those moments he needed someone, anyone. Once or twice, lately, she happened to have been the one who was on hand, but she would be crazy if she imagined that he felt anything for her, personally. She remembered the night when he had kissed her on the cliff-top, and she thought she understood, now, what it had all been about. Those cliffs had looked out towards Filfla, and on that summer night, staring out through the darkness, Peter had felt the horror of his loss all over again. She had been there, and instinctively he had turned to her, but only, undoubtedly, as he might have turned to any woman.

They reached Valletta just after one o'clock, and as Catriona extricated herself from the car she felt limp, exhausted and sticky with perspiration. More than once during the drive from Marsa Peter had asked her if she would like to stop for a drink, but by mutual consent they had carried on. Neither, she realised, had wanted that kind of tête-à-tête.

Back in the security of her own room, she took a quick, refreshing shower and tried not to think about the events of the morning. Toni was nowhere to be seen, and to her relief Carmen brought a light lunch up to her, sparing her the necessity of making an appearance in the dining-room. Because she didn't want her appetite questioned, even by Carmen, she made a real effort to eat, but the chicken salad stuck in her throat, and the fluffy lemon soufflé was even worse. Putting the tray outside her door, she soon closed the shutters and lay down, trying desperately to lose herself in sleep. But sleep refused to come, and for two hours she lay tossing and turning in the warm dimness, struggling with thoughts that refused to be kept at bay.

At half past four Toni tapped softly on her door, and when she came into the room Catriona tensed uneasily, terrified lest the other girl's sharp eyes should detect too much. It was difficult to answer a battery of searching questions without betraying details that she would prefer not to betray and almost impossible, without straying on to dangerous territory, to explain exactly how she had spent the morning. Somehow, though, she managed to come up with satisfactory answers, and mercifully it wasn't too long before the subject was exhausted. It was the boat crossing which appeared to interest Toni more than anything else—mainly, it seemed, because she had never been out in the new launch *Sultana*.

Catriona had expected her to be disappointed, because she had not been included in the Gozo expedition, but surprisingly the Maltese girl didn't seem to mind much. She had apparently spent a quiet morning sunbathing in the courtyard, and it was clear that she had been giving a good deal of thought to the evening ahead. No Maltese social event, it seemed, was more glamorous or romantic than an evening spent at Castel Verdala, and as Toni planned to dress accordingly she was anxious to know what Catriona would be wearing. Conscious of the fact that the English girl's wardrobe was more limited than her own, she was eager to help by lending one of her own dresses. After all, as she pointed out, they were almost the same size. But Catriona had borne enough humiliation for one day, and she was not going to appear before Peter Vilhena in plumage borrowed from his stepsister. She would not say so to Toni, at least not in so many words, but her refusal was very firm, and in the end Toni agreed reluctantly that the embroidered skirt would do perfectly well.

It took Toni some time to dress, but when she eventually emerged from her room she was looking lovelier than Catriona had ever seen her. Her hair, freshly washed, was a dusky cloud about her shoulders, and her diaphanous silk voile evening dress was the clear dark green of young hibiscus leaves. Her eyes were bright and sparkling, her skin glowed and her make-up was perfect. She had made a very special effort, and the result was so effective that when her brother saw her he actually nodded approvingly. He barely looked at Catriona. In fact, when they were all assembled in the courtyard he hardly seemed to notice her existence, but to her intense relief Toni made no comment.

Castel Verdala was a massive fortress of weathered stone which had been built at the end of the sixteenth century as a summer palace for the Grand Masters of the Order of St John, and it was surrounded by the most romantic gardens on the island. By the time they arrived, night was falling rapidly, and the castle, ablaze with light, was a fairy-tale palace. It had been

erected at the summit of a little hill, and on one side
its gardens sloped gently downwards to a wooded
valley, the Boschetto, which for hundreds of years
had been one of Malta's most celebrated beauty
spots. In the Boschetto, early Grand Masters had
hunted deer and gazelle. Tonight, golden lights
glimmered among the trees, and feminine laughter
echoed along the hidden paths.

The gardens were already crowded with people,
men in white dinner-jackets and women in glamorous dresses. Everywhere, couples were wandering
beneath the stars and new arrivals were greeting their
friends and acquaintances. Catriona was introduced
to several people, and as if from a great distance she
listened to their attempts at polite conversation. She
had never felt less like being social and after a time
she found herself longing for an opportunity to melt
into obscurity, to vanish into the shadow between the
trees.

The play began nearly half an hour late, but nobody seemed to mind. It was being staged on one of
the terraces, against a backcloth of golden stone, and
on either side pine trees crowded close. In such a setting *Twelfth Night* took on a rare and special magic,
and in spite of her aching unhappiness Catriona was
conscious of the fact that she was witnessing a performance worth remembering. The cast was good,
and she was forced to admit that Jacqueline made a
charming and convincing Olivia. The costume
suited her, and she looked stunningly beautiful, a
creature over whom any man might be expected to
lose his head. For the first time in her life Catriona
found herself wishing that she had been born beautiful and irresistible—a breathtaking Circe with limit-

less power over the whole of the male sex.

And yet. . . . She didn't want the whole of the male sex. She wanted just one man.

She saw Peter, seated near by, watching the stage with an expression on his face which she found hard to fathom. He was certainly attentive, and his eyes dwelt a lot on the lovely Jacqueline, but Catriona did not feel that he was particularly interested in the progress of the play. Toni, on the other hand, was enchanted by everything—by the actors, by the costumes, by the lyrical charm of the play itself. Catriona wondered, absently, where her boy-friend was, and whether in fact he still was her boy-friend. She seemed so happy, so carefree, so in love with life.

During the first interval Catriona remained in her seat. With formal courtesy Peter had asked if he could get her a drink, but she had refused and he had disappeared, no doubt to go in search of Jacqueline. Left alone, she stared at the empty stage and wondered how she was going to get through the remainder of the evening. That afternoon, her life had been changed by the feel of a man's arms about her, by the touch of his lips, and now she was being forced to spend an evening watching a theatrical performance by the woman who would one day most probably be his wife. She had no doubt that Peter intended to marry Jacqueline. And she hadn't much doubt that he wanted her to be aware of the fact.

Not far away, in the Italian garden, a string quartet had begun playing Mozart and she watched a full moon rise slowly above the encircling trees. She felt alone as she had never been in her life before, even on the day her mother finally left for the other side of the world. And yet all she wanted to do was to get as far away as possible from the sight and the sound and even the memory of Peter Vilhena. If she didn't do that soon, life would become unbearable. She had fallen in love with him; nothing could alter that. But he didn't want her. He didn't need her. And there was no possibility that he ever would.

In the morning, she would tell him that she had to go home. Toni didn't need her, not now, and it wouldn't be difficult to find an excuse that would satisfy the Maltese girl. And if Peter himself guessed the truth, she couldn't help it. Tears of humiliation stung behind her eyelids.

During the second interval Toni insisted on drawing her out into the throng of humanity clustering round the bar, and almost immediately she was seized upon by Paolo Sciberras, who told her that he had been trying, unsuccessfully, to contact her. He urged her to have a drink with him and she tried hard to think of an excuse for saying no. Glancing round, she told him she thought Toni might be looking for her, but he laughed and pointed the other girl out to her. Surrounded by an admiring group, Toni was testing out her own dramatic skill by declaiming some lines from the play, and she didn't look as if she was unduly concerned about the whereabouts of her English friend.

'You see?' Paolo said triumphantly. 'Now, come and have a drink.'

She shook her head, and was about to think of another excuse when she suddenly saw Peter. He was leaning against a stone balustrade, a glass in his hand, and he was staring straight at her. She stared back, then suddenly, hardly knowing what she was doing, she turned to Paolo.

'Thanks.' She smiled at him. 'I'm beginning to feel thirsty.'

He steered her towards the bar, and as they went she could feel Peter's eyes boring into her back. Firmly refusing anything stronger, she let Paolo buy her a tomato juice, and then she tried to listen attentively while he told her about his hopes of studying geology in America. He told her that he had made several attempts to get in touch with her that day, and as they talked she tried not to notice the eager glow in his dark eyes. He was a nice boy, but she certainly didn't want to encourage him. She was sorry she had let him buy her a drink.

When the interval was over she managed to persuade him that she really had to rejoin the Vilhenas, and reluctantly he let her go, assuring her that he would be on the phone the following morning.

Somewhere around eleven o'clock the play ended, to rapturous applause. All the actors seemed to be popular, but Jacqueline received a particularly wild ovation and as the floral tributes piled up around her feet she seemed to glow with satisfaction. She was born to be admired, Catriona thought wryly. She would never be happy away from the limelight Peter would have to remember that.

People began to move, most of them clustering together in groups, a few heading towards the car park. Toni hesitated for a moment, then she placed a hand on Catriona's arm.

'There is someone I must speak to. Do you mind?'

'Of course not.' Catriona sat down again, watching as Toni slipped gracefully through the crowd. Once again she was completely alone. She hadn't seen Peter since the second interval and she supposed he had found a seat closer to the stage. By this time, anyway, he would be with Jacqueline. She looked towards the darkened terrace which, until a few minutes ago had been the stage, and saw that all the actors and actresses had disappeared. By now they would be entertaining their families and friends. There would be toasts and congratulations, laughter and excited tributes. Husbands and wives would be there, boy-friends and girl-friends. Peter would be there.

She sighed, digging the toe of her shoe into a carpet of soft turf. At least she could be thankful for one thing—she had not been called upon to join the party congratulating Jacqueline.

One by one the floodlights and spotlights were turned off, and it wasn't long before the gardens were illuminated only by moonlight. The string quartet had gone and the bar had closed down, but there were still people lingering in the parterres and broad walks, shadowy figures, picturesque and unreal, and with detached interest Catriona watched them. Here and there, moonlight gleamed softly on a girl's hair or drew cold fire from a massive jewel. It was a tableau vivant more impressive than anything she had witnessed in the play itself, for these people were real. Tonight, in this enchanted, scented garden, they were living a part of their lives.

Gradually, though, everyone was drifting away, and she was beginning to feel conspicuous, even vaguely uneasy. There was no sign of Toni or of her brother, so when fifteen minutes had elapsed she decided to make her way towards the car park. It would be better, somehow, to wait by the car than to linger here in the gardens alone.

The car park was an extensive gravelled area capable of accommodating a very large number of vehicles, but by the time Catriona reached it there were barely ten or twelve cars left. She couldn't think where Toni had got to, and Mario had not come with them tonight. Peter was doing the driving himself. She caught sight of Gina and Paolo Sciberras, who were just getting into a rakish black-and-purple two-seater which had been parked next to the Citroën, and at sight of her Paolo looked startled.

'You are all alone?'

'Yes, I'm waiting for Toni and Count Vilhena.'

'Waiting for them? Where have they gone?'

Gina intervened rather hurriedly. 'I saw Antoinette a little while ago,' she confessed. 'She and Vittorio were going for a drive in his car. She said they would not be long.' She moved closer to Catriona. 'I didn't know she had left you alone, though. Where is Peter?'

'I think—well, one of the actresses is a close friend of his.'

Gina's eyes rolled upwards. 'Men are impossible! I suppose it's Jacqueline Calleja?'

'I think so.'

'Well, they cannot abandon you like this. Get into the car, we'll drive you home. Won't we, Paolo?'

'Of course,' Paolo agreed with alacrity. He looked as if he could hardly believe his good fortune.

Catriona shook her head. 'Thank you, but I must wait for Toni.'

'Why? She may be a long time, and you can't wait here alone,' he pointed out.

'I know that.'

While they were talking another two cars had

pulled out of the line, and she realised that once Gina and Paolo had gone, her situation might soon become rather unpleasant. Still, she couldn't leave—not, at least, without Toni. That would be impossible. And Toni was with Vittorio Falzon. Her uneasiness deepened.

'Where did they go?' she asked Gina. 'Have you any idea?'

Gina looked slightly uncomfortable. 'I don't know.'

'Well, why did they go?' Catriona heard her own voice rising and becoming faintly agitated.

Gina moved her slim shoulders expressively. 'Who knows? They are in love.'

Realisation hit Catriona with the violence of a cold douche. She actually believed that Toni had put Vittorio Falzon out of her mind, and all the time. . . . Another thought struck her, and she felt rather cold. That evening, while they were waiting for Peter, Toni had asked a lot more questions about the motor-launch *Sultana*. She didn't seem to have known, before, that her brother kept the boat moored at Marsa, and she wanted to hear all about it, even asking some fairly technical questions connected with the outboard motor. Catriona had been quite unable to answer them and assumed that she was interested only because she had been brought up among boats and boatbuilding. Now, a sudden fear swept over her. A wild thought entered her head and with a flash of intuition she decided that she knew what Toni was doing. She was sure, too, that she was right. She had no real doubts at all.

She looked through the dimness at Gina and her brother. 'I've got to follow her,' she said. 'I've got to.

But I can't drive.'

Gina looked blank. 'Why follow them? They just want to be alone, that's all.'

Catriona shook her head. 'I don't think so. I think it's more serious than that, a lot more serious.' She kept remembering Toni's unnatural composure and air of self-possession, the radiance she had exuded tonight. 'I believe. . . .' She hesitated, even now unwilling to say the words. 'I believe they may have been planning to run away together.'

'Planning to run away?' Gina sounded horrified. 'Oh no . . . no, it's not possible! Where would they go? They could not—no, it's quite impossible.'

'It might not be,' Catriona pointed out. 'If they took one of Count Vilhena's boats they could—well, I suppose they could make for Sicily.' She described the motor-launch that was moored at Marsa and the questions Toni had been asking.

'But Antoinette would not do this,' Gina protested again. 'Her brother would be so angry. And besides, it is very dangerous, I think.'

'I know it's dangerous,' Catriona said urgently. 'But I'm sure Toni would do it, unless Vittorio is the type to stop her.'

Gina looked a little less certain. 'Vittorio loves her. He would not wish to make her unhappy.'

'That's what I thought. And it really is vital to catch up with them as quickly as possible.'

Moving with more decision than she would have expected of him, Paolo held open the door of his little two-seater and indicated that his sister should scramble into the minute space behind the bucket seats. 'In that case we shall go and chase them, uh?'

For just a moment Catriona hesitated, wondering

whether or not she should try and contact Peter Vilhena. Then she pushed the idea out of her mind. Peter was with Jacqueline; there wasn't much doubt about that. He would hardly want his evening interrupted, and she certainly did not want to be responsible for the interruption. She might even be wrong about Toni and Vittorio, and even if she were not— well, with the help of Paolo and Gina there was no reason why she should not be able to handle the situation.

Noisily, Paolo reversed out of the line of cars, and within seconds they were on the road. The lanes near Castel Verdala were narrow and twisting and beyond the drystone walls there were dense thickets of carob and prickly pear which made it difficult to see very far ahead, even with the aid of moonlight, but in spite of everything they managed to make good progress. It was impossible to drive as fast as Paolo would probably have liked to drive, but even so they seemed to be doing about sixty miles an hour, and it wasn't long before Catriona found herself holding on to her seat with both hands. She felt faintly guilty about Gina, pushed unceremoniously into the back, but at the same time she was too worried about Toni to bother much about anything else. After about five minutes they emerged on to a fairly straight main road, and immediately Paolo put his foot down, flashing through tiny villages at frightening speed. Once, a thin, rangy cat crossed in front of them, its tortoiseshell markings vivid in the glare of the headlamps, and Catriona closed her eyes, terrified that it would be hit. But it crossed the road in safety and they hurtled onwards, the speedometer climbing steadily.

Once or twice, she knew, Paolo glanced at her in the darkness and she was vaguely conscious of the fact that he hoped she would be impressed by his driving, but she had no time to think of him. She was hardly aware that he existed. He was simply the means by which she might be able to prevent Toni doing something incredibly stupid and dangerous.

It took them nineteen minutes to reach Marsa, and as they roared down the hill to the wide open space behind the landing-stage she could see that a light burned on the jetty and a solitary car was parked beside the locked and abandoned café that normally served the ferry queue. There was no one about.

They all piled out of the car and without much delay Paolo identified the parked vehicle as belonging to Vittorio Falzon. Feeling that her worst fears had been realised, Catriona began running towards the Vilhenas' private landing-stage, the others behind her, and as she ran she tried to think. She didn't really know what she would say if and when they caught up with Toni and Vittorio, but she had no doubt in her mind that it would be possible to stop them. Toni was sensible—she would listen.

She ran past the boathouse, Paolo close behind her now. Low down, near the horizon, there was a bank of lowering cloud, but the moon was still riding clear and the shore was bathed in silver light. Breathlessly, Catriona turned the corner. The boathouse doors were wide and with the exception of a few tools there was nothing inside. She walked to the edge of the jetty and looked down at the water. Dark, shining water lapped almost soundlessly against the steps. She could see the iron ring to which the *Sultana* had been moored that afternoon, and it seemed to mock her. Biting her lip in bitter frustration, she stared out across the moonlit sea, but there was nothing in sight. Though she strained her ears, there was no sound of an outboard motor.

Paolo came up behind her. 'They had a good start on us,' he pointed out. 'It's a calm night and with a good engine they could be a long way away by now.'

'It's calm so far,' said Catriona. Her voice was small and tight. 'But those clouds. . . .'

Gina appeared round a corner of the boathouse, carrying one fragile silver sandal.

'My tights are torn,' she complained, 'and I think my heel is broken. I am very angry with Antoinette.'

Sinking down on the stones of the jetty, she examined her damaged shoe, then glanced at the other two. 'She has gone, I suppose?'

Through the stillness of the night there came the distant hum of an engine and for a moment Catriona glanced hopefully out to sea. Perhaps—could they be coming back? Then as the sound grew louder she realised that it came from the road behind them. It was the sound of a car approaching fast and as its headlamps swung into view she knew instinctively who was driving it.

The Citroën stopped with a squeal of brakes and almost in the same moment Peter swung himself out of the driving-seat. He was alone, and they all three stared at him. How could he have known?

He strode rapidly towards them over the uneven ground and Catriona saw that his face was pale and taut in the moonlight. 'You were too late,' he remarked tersely, as he caught up with them. 'They put to sea half an hour ago.'

'How did you know?' Catriona asked helplessly.

'I was told that my sister had left the gardens with Falzon and also that you,' he looked at Catriona, 'had been seen driving off with Gina and Paolo. I guessed that you had thought it necessary to go in search of Antoinette, and then an idea occurred to me, so I telephoned the police station here.' He nodded towards a small lighted building a couple of hundred yards away to their left. 'The Sergeant told me that my launch had put to sea a few minutes earlier. He was not worried at the time because he knew the boat was fitted with a variety of alarms. Whoever took her obviously understood the system, so he assumed it must be all right.'

'Does Toni understand the alarms?'

'Yes. Last summer, when she was here, she enjoyed playing with a similar security system which had been fitted to another of our boats. Anyway, Sergeant Mifsud believes the *Sultana* was taken by a man and a girl, so there doesn't seem to be much doubt. He has been put in possession of the facts and the rescue services have been alerted, together with the excise patrol boats for this area.'

Catriona looked at him, a question in her eyes. 'Rescue services?'

He nodded towards the thickening cloud bank. 'That's coming closer, and it may affect conditions.'

Catriona swallowed. Despite the sticky warmth of the night she felt cold, and her body seemed to ache with sympathy for Peter. She thought of Marina, broken all those years ago on the rocks of Filfla, and understood what he must be going through.

Gina looked frightened. 'They'll be all right, won't they? They'll be brought back?'

Peter turned away from them. 'There's no point in

hanging about here.' He glanced over his shoulder at Paolo. 'I'm very grateful to you, Sciberras, but there's nothing more you can do. You had better take your sister home.'

Paolo nodded soberly. He looked at Catriona. 'I'll telephone you in the morning.'

'All right,' she said absently. 'If you like.'

As they moved back towards the cars, Peter turned round to look once more at the glistening sea. 'I hope they're all right, out there.'

'So do I,' she answered, moistening dry lips.

Paolo and Gina drove away almost immediately, but for a moment or two Peter sat very still behind the wheel of the Citroën. Then he extracted a bundle of maps and charts from the glove compartment.

'Where do you think they've gone?' Catriona asked at last, her voice husky.

'Sicily.' With the aid of a torch, he studied one of the charts more closely.

'How far is it?'

'Too far.' His voice was toneless. 'They won't make it.'

'Not—not even if the weather holds?'

He shook his head. 'No.' Then he stiffened, listening. From far out over the sea there came a faint ominous growl of thunder.

Catriona shivered, and she saw Peter's lips tighten.

'Wait here,' he said abruptly. 'I shan't be long.'

He got out of the car, taking the torch with him and as he closed the door on her and walked away into the darkness she felt a sudden panic-stricken urge to follow him. But she didn't. Instead, she sat very still, willing herself to stay calm. She knew that he needed her support and she wasn't going to let him down. Of course, Jacqueline should have been with him, but naturally she would still be celebrating the success of her first night. It probably wouldn't have been possible to drag her away. Perhaps she didn't even know what was going on. With iron determination, Catriona forced herself to be fair, at least in her own mind. At the very thought of Jacqueline, she felt cold and sick with jealousy, but she mustn't let her judgment be affected by that. She mustn't.

Glancing in the driving mirror, she saw that Peter was walking towards the police station and supposed he was going to ask for advice or information. Perhaps they would have something to tell him already? She looked out of the window, noticing that the moon was beginning to slip behind the advancing cloud bank. Thunder rolled again, a little nearer this time, and she clenched her fingers to stop them trembling. The sea looked very dark now, dark and vaguely menacing. How could Toni have done such a crazy thing? What chance did they stand? Had Vittorio Falzon talked her into it, or had it been her own idea?

Looking back over the last few days she could see, now, that they might have met again and again. Probably they had been together at Gina's party, and there must have been many other occasions when brief meetings would have been possible. She didn't know why she had been taken in, why she had ever imagined they would give up so easily. If she had been in the same position and Peter had loved her as Vittorio apparently loved Toni, would she have given him up?

The moon disappeared completely, and suddenly it was very dark. Spots of rain appeared on the windscreen and thunder growled again. She looked at the digital clock on the dashboard and saw that it was ten minutes past twelve. Toni and Vittorio had now been at sea for something like three-quarters of an hour. How far would they have got?

Firm footsteps sounded beside the car and Peter unlocked the door. Without saying anything he got in and started the engine. They turned, the headlamps showing that it was now raining quite hard, and then they moved off along the road that led back towards Valletta.

Glancing at Peter, Catriona saw that his face was grim. 'What did they say?' she asked.

'That the storm is getting worse,' he answered briefly.

'Is that all? How long will it be before they trace the *Sultana*?'

'I have no idea.' He frowned. 'I spoke by telephone to Falzon's father. He tells me his son has no boating experience whatsoever.'

She looked at him anxiously. 'Toni has, though—hasn't she?'

He shrugged. 'She has been taken out many times, yes. But I wouldn't trust her to take charge of a rubber dinghy.'

Catriona had a thought. 'Isn't there any way they can be contacted?'

He shook his head. 'The *Sultana* has no radio.'

She sensed that he didn't want to talk, but she had to say something. 'Where are we going now?'

'Back to Valletta.' He glanced at the dashboard clock. 'We should be there in ten minutes' time, and you can then go quietly to bed.'

She looked horrified. 'I couldn't go to bed! Not until I know they're safe.'

'No? Well, you must do as you like,' he said rather harshly.

'You'll be sitting up, waiting for news,' she pointed out. 'Can't I—can't I wait with you?'

'No, you cannot.' His voice was sharp and impatient. 'For one thing, I shall not be sitting up, waiting for news. I have a fast cruiser moored in St Paul's Bay and when I've disposed of you I shall take her out and join the search. Assuming, of course, that they have not been found.'

Catriona felt a jolt in the pit of her stomach. Naturally, he'd want to do that. He'd have to. She should have realised.

'Well,' she said positively, 'you mustn't waste time taking me back to Valletta. I'll wait in the car, if you like, but—but I wish you'd let me go with you.'

'Let you. . . .' He sounded outraged. 'Santa Maria! You're not serious?'

'Of course I am.' She felt tears rising in her throat, threatening to choke her, preventing her from speaking clearly. 'I'm very fond of Toni,' she said, floundering desperately. 'I want to know what's happening.' As he remained silent, she added, 'Please—please let me go with you. I won't be a nuisance, and I won't get in your way. I'm not nervous, and if the worst comes to the worst I'm a strong swimmer.' She stopped, wondering if she had said too much.

Peter was silent for a long moment, then he shrugged. 'Very well, as you wish. On such an occasion I would not choose to burden myself with unnecessary female company but it will certainly save time.' He glanced at her. 'What about your clothes?'

'They don't matter, and they're quite comfortable.' Well, at least her skirt was not long and mercifully she was wearing flat-heeled Roman sandals. She might not be dressed very suitably for putting to sea in a motor-cruiser, but at least her clothes would not hamper her.

When they reached St Paul's Bay it was very quiet, and there was no one about as they parked the car and made their way down towards the harbour. Twenty or thirty yachts and cruisers were moored side by side, and in the pale light from a solitary street lamp they looked a little like ghost ships. Peter's was one of the largest, a gleaming white vessel bearing the name *Khamsin*, and as Catriona clambered aboard she wondered fleetingly whether this were another product of the Gozo boatyard. She certainly seemed to have been fitted out to meet the requirements of a discriminating owner, for her main cabin was equipped with everything from an elaborate hi-fi system to a bookcase full of books, and there was even a businesslike writing desk with a range of lockers below it.

The rain had eased a little and the storm still seemed to be a long way off, but curtly Peter told Catriona to go below and because she was determined not to be a nuisance, she obeyed. A minute or two later he came down and told her that he had been in touch by radio with the rescue services and that there was still no news. So far the *Sultana* had not been sighted.

Catriona looked at him anxiously. 'Does that mean anything?' she asked.

'It probably means they're off course, which is

only to be expected.' He eyed her without enthusiasm. 'I don't know why you have to be here, but since you are you had better do as you're told. I want you to stay below. If I have anything to say to you I'll use the intercom.'

She nodded dumbly and as he disappeared up the narrow companionway she sat down, staring at the complicated dials of the stereo, telling herself that she should have been prepared for the stony dislike in his eyes. He didn't want her around. Probably he even resented her presence. Jacqueline should have been with him, if it had been possible.

A little later the engine sprang to life and the whole boat shuddered violently. A widening band of water appeared between them and the harbour wall, and she saw the shore lights begin to slip past. They swung round, heading out to sea, and Catriona went through into the vibrating galley, where she found a coffee percolator. A further search produced coffee, sugar and powdered milk, and she set about filling the percolator. It gave her something to do. Almost it made her feel useful. She thought of Peter, up above, standing at the wheel, and wondered what sort of thoughts were running through his head. He must be remembering Marina.

The percolator heated quickly, and when she had poured the coffee into mugs she climbed the companionway. Peter's head and shoulders were silhouetted against the *Khamsin*'s shining white superstructure, and at sight of him her heart lurched. He had a strong profile and no man could have looked more confident or more firmly in control. And yet. . . .

She offered him a mug of coffee and he took it

without looking at her.

'Go back,' he said tersely. 'Stay below, as I told you.'

'Couldn't I. . . .' Her voice was pleading. 'Couldn't I stay up here, just for a little while?'

He said nothing for nearly half a minute, then he made a small dismissive gesture. 'If you like.'

Catriona sat down close to him, watching his strong, capable hands as they turned the wheel a fraction. The lights of St Paul's were retreating rapidly and ahead lightening glimmered on the horizon. Far away, the storm growled again.

'I thought you were afraid of thunder,' Peter said quietly.

'I was.' She looked at the lightning flickering in the distance. 'Somehow, it doesn't seem so bad any more.'

He laughed suddenly, harshly. 'You mean that particular phobia has served its purpose.'

She felt puzzled. 'What do you mean?'

'Well, it did precipitate quite a touching little scene, didn't it?'

Catriona bit her lip, so fiercely that it began to bleed. Surely he didn't think. . . . Her cheeks burned, and as she stood up she opened her mouth to say something, but no words would come. When she did speak her voice sounded strangled and unnatural.

'I'm sorry, I shouldn't have asked you to bring me with you tonight. It must be so embarrassing. After all, I might start throwing myself at you. At any moment, really. Of course, I haven't had a lot of practice, but—but as you can see, I'm working at it.' She broke off and stumbled unseeingly towards the companionway. Somehow she made her way down

into the galley, desperate to get as far away from
Peter as possible. She tried a door at the far end of
the cabin and when it yielded found herself in a well
planned stateroom, panelled in pine and with a
carpet into which her sandalled feet sank deeply. Her
fumbling fingers found the light switch and she
slammed the door behind her, then, hardly knowing
what she was doing, she sat down on the wide bed
and clasped her arms about her own trembling body.
Several minutes went by while she sat there, trying
without much success to control the waves of misery
that engulfed her.

At last the door opened, and Peter stood on the
threshold. 'What the hell are you doing?' he demanded roughly. He came in, closing the door
behind him.

'Leave me alone.' Catriona stood up, backing
away from him. 'Please!'

'Pull yourself together,' he said sharply. 'I can't
leave the wheel for long.' He stopped, staring at her.
Her grey eyes were dark with hurt, and her face was
very pale beneath its light golden tan. Her small
breasts, thinly veiled by the shell-pink silk, were
heaving with suppressed sobs. There was blood on
her lips.

'Catriona!' His voice softened miraculously and he
moved towards her.

She drew back, retreating before him as if he were
some sort of monster, but he caught both her hands
and held them tightly. 'Look at me,' he commanded.

Wordlessly, she shook her head, but releasing one
of her hands, he captured her chin and forced it
upwards.

'Let me go,' she pleaded. 'I hate you. Do you

understand? I hate you!'

'No, no,' he said softly. 'No, you don't.' His arms went round her, and as he drew her close to him she tried to struggle. But his strength was too great and his touch turned her knees to water. He was forcing her head back and there was nothing she could do. His mouth came down, devouring hers, and with a gesture of helpless surrender she wound her arms around his neck. The kiss seemed to last for a very long time, and when it ended he lowered her gently on to the bed.

'Catriona——' Softly, he whispered her name again. His lips found her throat, sending shivers of ecstasy through her, and his fingers began tugging gently at her shoulder-straps.

Catriona pressed her cheek to his smooth black hair and wondered dizzily if she could be dreaming. She wasn't even sure, any longer, exactly where they were. It was enough that they were together. Her blood was on fire and she knew that she wanted him just as much as he wanted her.

And then their private world was invaded by a curious crackling sound. Staccato and irritating, the sound persisted until it resolved itself into something remarkably like a voice. Slowly, Peter lifted his head and she realised he was listening. Very, very gently, he relaxed his hold on her and with one lithe movement swung himself off the bed. Striding out of the cabin, he left the door swinging behind him.

When Catriona joined him on deck, five minutes later, she was making a tremendous effort not to betray any sort of emotion. Peter, she knew, had been listening to a radio message, and despite the turmoil going on inside her she, too, wanted to know what it had contained. Thunder still rumbled in the distance, but the rain had stopped and she saw at once that they had put on speed. Peter, once again standing at the wheel, looked cool and alert. He spoke without looking round.

'Some trawler has reported a small motor-boat heading at full speed towards the north coast of Gozo. Three patrol boats are heading for the area, but I plan to be there before them.'

'Do you think—do you think it's Toni and Vittorio?' Catriona asked hesitantly.

'Yes.'

'Well, if they're heading towards Gozo they'll be all right, won't they? I mean, they must be planning to go ashore.'

'I daresay they are planning to go ashore,' he said grimly. 'Unfortunately, they've picked the wrong coast. It's a mass of murderous rocks. They won't stand a chance.'

Catriona caught her breath. 'Wouldn't Toni know about the rocks?'

He shook his head. 'I doubt if she even realises they're heading for Gozo. She probably imagines they've reached Sicily. By this time, in any case, she'll be panic-stricken. They might as well be adrift.'

'Surely——' She hesitated. 'Vittorio must have some sense.'

'According to his father, he knows nothing about boats. He isn't likely to learn under these conditions.'

Catriona was silent. Her body still throbbed with the life breathed into it by his kisses, and she longed to touch his cheek, to cover his hand with her own— to comfort him through the depths of her love. But he had drawn away from her again and this time he seemed to have moved a thousand miles away.

Then the clouds covering the moon thinned. Suddenly she saw the outline of Gozo, and it was much closer than she had expected. They were cutting through the water at tremendous speed, leaving twin trails of foam behind them, and Peter seemed to be steering straight for the cliffs.

Catriona peered into the blackness. 'Oughtn't we to see lights?' she asked.

'No,' he said shortly. 'We're making for the deserted north coast.'

She moved closer to the rail. Already she could see waves creaming at the foot of the cliffs, but nothing else. There was no sign of another boat, no hint of life. They seemed to be alone on the surface of the world.

Then she felt as if her heart stood still. About a quarter of a mile away, on the starboard side, she had glimpsed a green navigation light. The light was moving almost as fast as they were and it, too, was heading towards Gozo.

At that moment the moon sailed completely clear, and for the first time she saw the rocks, jagged and menacing, glistening as the sea washed over them.

'Get below,' Peter said sharply. His eyes narrowed as he stared into the darkness, and she realised they were altering course, veering towards the launch.

'That's the *Sultana*, isn't it?' Catriona felt frozen, incapable of movement.

'Yes.'

'Why are they heading straight for the rocks? Why don't they. . . .'

'The logic of their behaviour is beyond me. Now, go below!'

'Please. . . .' There was urgent appeal in her voice. 'I want to stay here. I want to know what's happening.'

Peter didn't look at her. 'As you wish,' he said at last.

She stared at the dimly visible outline of the launch. 'Can't you signal them? There must be something. . . .'

'No. A signal would confuse them.'

They were racing through the water now, hurtling at frightening speed towards the tall cliffs. Like a powerful bird they passed the *Sultana*, and then—Catriona's fingers gripped the rail. They were not going to slacken speed.

She stared straight ahead, bracing herself for the moment when the *Khamsin* would be thrown on to those malevolent black teeth. Wildly, she thought that perhaps this was the way Peter wanted it. Perhaps it was even the best way.

Above the roar of the engine she heard his voice, raw and savage.

'If you won't go below, hang on!'

They turned, so sharply that she was thrown hard against the rail. Cold spray cascaded over her, drenching her hair, and she felt the roughness of salt on her lips. The cliffs loomed over her, shutting out the sky and then drew away again. They swung in a half-circle, missing vicious rocks by yards, and through a haze of flying spray she glimpsed the *Sultana*. Then she heard Peter's voice again.

'Slow down, you blasted fools!'

Suddenly she realised what was happening. Peter

was doing the only thing possible. He was trying to check the little motor-boat's headlong progress by throwing the *Khamsin* in front of her.

Pushing wet hair out of her eyes, Catriona clung tightly to the rail, trying to see what was happening.

She realised, dazedly, that Peter was cutting back the engine. Their own speed was dropping and the world was no longer revolving round them. Through the moist darkness she saw the cliffs of Gozo, farther away than they had been—and then she saw the *Sultana*.

Perhaps fifty yards from the treacherous shore, Toni and Vittorio had brought their craft to a halt.

Stunned and trembling a little, Catriona relaxed her hold on the rail. Her fingers were raw, and she felt icy cold. She hardly realised what was happening —until Peter appeared and carried her below.

CHAPTER ELEVEN

A BLANKET round her shoulders, Catriona watched from a porthole as the *Sultana* was taken in tow. Having deposited her unceremoniously in the cabin, Peter had ordered her to stay there and keep warm, and this time she had neither the strength nor the spirit to disobey. Outside, three newly-arrived patrol boats were standing by, and temporarily the *Khamsin* seemed to be at anchor, for the black waters lapping her sides were as quiet as an island pool. Catriona could hear voices, Toni's among them, and see vague movements, but it wasn't until she heard heavy footsteps on the deck overhead that she knew for certain the runaways had been taken aboard. Moments later, the cabin door opened and Toni came in.

She was wearing jeans and a T-shirt—where, Catriona wondered, had she managed to change?—and she looked rather tired. Her black hair was damp, plastered to her head and there was a streak of oil across her cheek. At the sight of Catriona she looked startled and relieved. Possibly, Catriona thought, Toni imagined her brother would not be too violently angry in front of Catriona. If so, it seemed likely that she was being over-confident.

With mild interest she studied the young man who had followed Toni into the cabin. He was tall and good-looking, with thick, wavy hair and a humorous mouth. His eyes were anxious when they rested on Toni, and she decided he looked rather nice. She hoped things would somehow work out for them.

Outside, there was a sudden revving of engines, and the *Khamsin* rocked gently, caught in the wake of a departing patrol-boat. Peter came into the cabin, closing the door behind him. He looked dangerously calm.

'Well!' he said in English. 'Tonight we could all have been killed, but that I suppose I must disregard. I shall not disregard the fact that the *Sultana*'s engine is badly damaged. To whom shall I send the bill, Falzon—to you, or to my sister?'

'I shall pay,' Vittorio said quietly. He put an arm round Toni's shoulders. 'Would it be possible for Antoinette to have some strong coffee? She is still suffering from shock.'

'Of course.' Catriona took the blanket from her own shoulders and placed it round Toni's, at the same time giving the other girl's arm a reassuring squeeze. She began making some more coffee, and Peter shot her a curious look.

'We thought we were near Siracusa,' Toni said suddenly. There was the merest hint of a sob in her voice. 'I know such a safe place there—and it looks almost the same.'

'Unfortunately, though, it is not the same,' her stepbrother remarked dryly. 'There are ways of telling the difference, but they involve paying a certain amount of attention to navigation. Naturally, navigation has little to do with an elopement.'

Vittorio stood up. 'Count Vilhena, I very much regret having taken your boat. I apologise.'

Peter's eyebrows shot up. 'Really? What about my sister—how do you feel about taking her?'

'I regret that also.'

'Vittorio!' Toni's eyes opened wide, and she stared at him in pitiful, childlike disbelief.

'I must say,' Peter remarked evenly, 'your ardour cools with remarkable speed.'

'You misunderstand me, *signur*. I love Antoinette and intend to marry her, but I should not have exposed her to the difficulties and—and dangers of an escape to Sicily. She has a right to be married here in Malta, among her friends.'

Toni slipped her hand into his.

'My sister is eighteen years old,' the Count remarked. 'Before she can be married she will require her father's permission.'

'Your permission, I think you mean, *signur*.'

'In his absence, yes . . . mine.'

'Then I hope you will give it.'

Emerging from the galley, Catriona handed out steaming mugs of coffee. Toni shivered a little and clasped hers with both hands.

'Peter. . . .' Her voice was very small. 'I love him, more than anything in the world.'

'I should hope so,' her brother responded. 'I imagine you would not be likely to abscond in an open boat with a man to whom you were indifferent.'

'Then let me marry him.'

The Count turned to Vittorio. 'My principal objection, Falzon, is to your family. Your cousin. . . .'

Unable to bear it any longer, Catriona intervened. 'Surely,' she said urgently, 'you must see Vittorio is not in the least like his cousin? He's an entirely different sort of person. Everything he says makes it clear that—that he deserves to marry Toni.'

A flicker of amusement appeared in Peter's eyes. 'What a cryptic observation,' he remarked. He looked at his stepsister. Fortified by the coffee, she was showing signs of getting angry, but it was fairly obvious that she was being prevented from speaking by the warning grip of Vittorio's fingers.

'Very well!' the Count said suddenly. 'You may marry her, Falzon. I only ask that you do so quickly, since I am anxious to be relieved of such a tiresome responsibility.'

For a moment there was silence in the cabin. Then Toni hurled herself at her stepbrother, flinging her arms around his neck. Catriona saw Vittorio's face quiver and thought she understood how he must have been feeling a few moments earlier. She smiled at him.

'Congratulations! I know you're both going to be very happy.'

The next instant Toni was hugging her convulsively. 'Catriona, thank you!'

'I didn't do anything,' Catriona said a little wryly.

Peter interrupted unexpectedly. 'Oh, yes, you did.' His tone was dry and when she looked at him his look was inscrutable. 'I must give Miss Browne a job in one of my Sicilian quarries after the way she has softened my stony heart.'

Involuntarily she looked at him, but his eyes were cool and remote. Only half an hour earlier they had been on the point of making love—now that memory had acquired the quality of an elusive dream.

Twenty minutes later, in the first light of dawn, they all landed at the Gozitan port of Mgarr. The launch, apparently, was going to need repairs on Gozo, and it seemed that the *Khamsin*, too, had sustained damage which made her owner reluctant to go straight back to Malta. Tired and dazed, Catriona

stared unseeingly in front of her as a taxi took them
all to a luxury hotel on the cliff-top, and when they
checked in she hardly realised what was happening.
The hotel was an elaborate modern building, vaguely
reminiscent of a Sultan's palace, and under normal
circumstances the night porter would undoubtedly
have been reluctant, without special authority, to
admit bedraggled refugees from an incident at sea.
Count Vilhena, however, was another matter, and
when he explained that he had been obliged, unexpectedly, to abandon his motor-cruiser the staff
could not do enough. Four of the best bedrooms were
immediately made available and the hotel shop was
unlocked so that the Count's friends could provide
themselves with toothbrushes, though Toni, it turned
out, had a suitcase with her.

Several days earlier the case had been secreted in
Vittorio's car, and from it she had extracted the jeans
and T-shirt which she had worn for her abortive
elopement. She was able to lend Catriona a nightdress, and for a few minutes the two girls talked,
mainly about Toni's forthcoming wedding. It was
nearly four o'clock when Catriona finally made her
way to her own room and as she paused outside the
door she found herself wondering where Peter was.
He had not spoken to her since they came ashore.

The bedroom was large and comfortable, with
cream-washed walls and brightly coloured furnishings. At one end there was a massive television set, and
at the other wide glass doors looked out across a
verandah to the cliff-top and the sea. Through the
doors, which were standing open, cool morning air
drifted into the room, and in the pale light Catriona
began to undress slipping at last out of her embroid-

ered skirt. She felt battered and bruised in mind and body, but at the same time she was almost too tired and dazed to know why. In the small adjoining bathroom she took a shower, then she got into Toni's nightdress and lay down on the wide bed. Within seconds she was fast asleep.

When she awoke it was broad daylight, but there was something about the light that puzzled her. The room was very warm, and a mosquito was humming monotonously, close to her ear. She sat up, brushing the mosquito away, and looked at her watch, which had stopped. She wondered what the time could be.

She picked up the telephone and spoke to a polite young man in the reception office.

'Could you tell me the time, please?'

'Of course, madam. It's just after six o'clock.'

Catriona looked at the window. 'Six o'clock in the morning?'

The reception clerk laughed. 'No, six o'clock in the evening.'

'But it can't. . . .' Something like panic began to spread through her. 'I must have been asleep all day!'

'That's right, madam. Count Vilhena said you were not to be disturbed.'

'Is he still here? Count Vilhena, I mean.'

'No, he's gone back to Malta. He asked us to send him your bill.'

'Oh!' Catriona swallowed. She felt slightly sick. 'What—what about the others? Miss Caruana and Mr Falzon?'

'They went with him, madam.'

'I—I see.' She tried to sound natural. 'Was there

. . . was there any message for me?'

'I don't think so. I'll check if you like.' The clerk hesitated. 'Wouldn't you like something sent to your room? Some sandwiches, perhaps? Dinner will not begin until half past seven.'

'No, thanks. I—in a little while I'll come and get something.'

'Very well, madam.'

She hung up, staring blankly in front of her. Then, slowly, she swung her legs to the ground and stood up. She didn't need to wonder what Peter was trying to tell her. It was all too agonisingly obvious. He wanted to make it absolutely clear, once and for all, that there was nothing between them and never could be. Twice, the day before, he had yielded to a passing temptation. But she had no place in his life, and he obviously felt it was time she was made to understand. He had serious plans—plans that involved Jacqueline Calleja.

Forcing herself to behave sensibly, Catriona bathed and slipped into the cool dress lent to her by Toni, then she combed her hair and applied a little make-up. She felt as if her senses were numbed and she tried to remember something she had once said to Peter. *When things are very black . . . you just have to keep putting one foot in front of the other.* She was going to follow her own advice, for there was nothing else she could do, but the blankness ahead frightened her. She must try and concentrate on work—on getting back to England and catching up with preparations for the exhibition. That at least was something to cling to.

A wave of despair swept over her and she buried her head in her hands. No amount of work, no amount of success would ever make up to her for losing Peter.

'Good evening.' The voice was only too familiar.

She jumped, thinking her imagination was playing tricks on her. Slowly she turned her head—and then she saw him. He was standing on the verandah, outside her window, and he must have been watching her, probably for several minutes.

She stood up, her heart thumping so loudly that she thought he must be able to hear it.

'I—I thought you were in Malta.'

'I was, half an hour ago. Now, however, I appear to be here. I must apologise for approaching your bedroom in this unconventional manner, but it seemed the most direct way of getting to see you.'

'I've been asleep all day,' she told him.

'I know. I left instructions that you were not to be disturbed. I thought you would probably need time to recover from your adventures of last night.'

Recollecting what had happened during the previous night, she flushed scarlet, but he didn't seem to notice.

'Antoinette has spent the day in Valletta,' he remarked conversationally. 'I gather she has been looking at engagement rings and getting to know her fiancé's family. When they are married I have no doubt that she will cost young Vittorio a good deal of money, but fortunately he can afford it. His family are extremely wealthy.'

'They're very happy,' Catriona said. Though she didn't realise it, her voice sounded flat. 'It was good of you to agree, in the end.'

'I had little alternative,' he remarked wryly. 'Still, I am optimistic about Vittorio. He may quite possibly be able to control Antoinette, in which case he will have my profound respect. She is a little young for marriage, but on the other hand she is one of those women who badly need the stabilising influence of a husband.' He looked at her thoughtfully. 'What are your own plans?' he asked casually. 'Or are they too private to be discussed?'

She walked past him, out on to the verandah. This was the supreme test. Somehow she had to control her feelings, to prevent him guessing for an instant at the misery churning inside her.

'I have a lot of work to do,' she said. 'I can't wait to get back to it.'

'Your stay here in Malta has not been entirely unproductive. This morning, Antoinette showed me one of your paintings.'

'She did?' Catriona was startled.

'Yes. You must forgive her. I particularly wanted to see a sample of your work.' There was a pause, then he went on: 'I have quite a number of friends in the London art world, and I may be able to help you in some way.'

'That's very good of you.'

'Not at all.' He moved closer to her. 'I suppose, now, I must ask how soon you would like to leave us. Naturally, you will want to get back to London as quickly as possible, and it will be necessary for me to arrange your flight. How about the day after to-morrow? There's a Trident leaving at ten-thirty in the morning. Of course, if you would prefer not to wait so long?'

Catriona tried to speak, but to her horror realised that she couldn't. She dared not trust her voice. Silently Peter waited, while it seemed to her that minutes ticked away. Then he spoke again, very quietly.

'Aren't you going to say something, Catriona?'

'I . . . I. . . .' She gulped and was forced to stop. Colour flooded into her face and then receded. She looked away from him, then to her horror, she burst into tears.

'I shall have to say it, then.' His voice was very soft. 'You are not going anywhere, Catriona. I need you and you need me. We are two parts of one whole —indivisible.'

She looked up at him, blinking back the treacherous tears. 'What do you mean?' she asked huskily. And then her eyes met his and she began to feel she was drowning in something she still didn't quite understand.

'I mean that I love you,' he said.

His arms, as they closed around her, were like steel bands and when his mouth took possession of hers she felt as if sunlight were spreading inside her. For her, he was like the sun. Without him there was no warmth anywhere.

'You can't love me,' she murmured uncertainly, as soon as she was free to speak. 'You said. . . .'

'I know what I said.' He kissed her eyelids and the tip of her nose, then rested his cheek against her hair. 'When Marina was killed, I died too . . . or thought I did. For twelve years I sincerely believed that in some respects my life was over, that I could never love another woman. But then you came along, with your courage and honesty,'—he kissed her again, lingeringly—'and I didn't know what to do about you. Yesterday, I was hovering on the brink. I wanted to accept the fact that I loved you, but I didn't think it could be true. I thought I would suddenly wake up and discover that what I felt was just a mirage after all. In which case I knew I must not involve you in any way. But then last night I realised how much you meant to me, and suddenly it was all so simple. You see, you are everything I could ever want. If I don't have you I shall die again and this time it will be the end.' He drew back a little, gazing down into her face. '*Babuha*. . . .' His voice was anxious. 'You feel something for me, don't you? You love me a little?'

'I've shown you what I feel.' Catriona confessed, her face hidden against his shoulder. 'You're everything to me — everything in the world. No one in my life has ever mattered so much. I don't think I could live without you. I . . . I thought I was going to die when you talked about sending me back to England. . . .' She broke off, and as he kissed her again she wound her arms around his neck. The kiss lasted for a long time and when at last he lifted his head they still clung together.

'When will you marry me?' he asked, playing with the ends of her hair. 'It must be soon. I will not wait, my love.'

She smiled. Against his lips, she murmured, 'what about Jacqueline? I thought you planned to marry her.'

'Jacqueline?' He looked surprised. 'I would never have married her. She was—just a woman, someone to keep the boredom at bay. And she knew it. Besides, her career is everything to her and when she does marry she will probably pick the kind of man who can be useful to her.'

'It's funny.' Catriona sighed contentedly. 'Last

night I was so jealous of her that I could hardly watch the play.'

'*You* were jealous? How do you imagine I felt when I saw you drinking with Sciberras?'

'You minded?' She looked up at him, wide-eyed. 'You were jealous of Paolo?'

'Of course. I was out of my mind with jealousy. Why do you think I behaved so badly when we first boarded the *Khamsin*? I said terrible things to you then. . . .'

'Yes,' she agreed, 'you did.'

'Well, it was only because of Paolo. That afternoon I had held you in my arms and you had seemed to respond to me. Then suddenly I saw you with him and I could not endure it. I spent the rest of the evening pacing up and down in the Boschetto, annoying the birds, who were trying to sleep.'

'But I thought——' She looked up at him wonderingly. 'After the play, I thought you must be with Jacqueline.'

He shook his head. 'I was too busy getting angry with you and Paolo. It hurt so much—and later on, when I thought about it. . . .' He broke off. 'Have you forgiven me?'

Catriona tilted her head back so that she could look up at him more easily. 'I'll forgive you,' she said softly. 'But, Peter, love me always, won't you? And trust me.'

The sun was getting low, now, and its golden light fell full on her upturned face. Bending his head, he kissed her again. 'When we are married,' he murmured, 'you will be flesh of my flesh, and bone of my bone. We shall not be two people any more. Does that answer you?'

'Yes.' She ran her fingers through the crisp dark hair at the nape of his neck. 'Peter, I love you . . . I want to make you so happy.'

'You're making me happy now, and you always will. We shall both be so happy that other people will find us unbearable. We shall spend several months of every year at Ghajn Lucia—there is a nursery there which needs filling up.'

'Ghajn Lucia?' She looked up at him quickly, blushing at his meaning. 'You mean you'll open the house up?'

'Of course. I want you to love it as much as I do.'

Twenty minutes later they walked into the hotel foyer hand in hand, and a sudden thought flashed across her mind. 'Peter, my exhibition—it doesn't seem to matter any more. Do you think that's dreadful?'

He smiled at the top of her head. 'If it did matter, I would be worried.'

'But the people behind it—— They've been so kind.'

'Ask them to come out here,' he answered promptly. 'Don't worry, I'll make it up to them.'

'You mustn't spoil me.'

He smiled, his eyes dark with tenderness. 'I couldn't do that.'

'Let's ring Toni,' she said suddenly. 'I want her to know how wonderful everything is.'

Standing still in the middle of the foyer, Peter looked down at her for a moment. Then he lifted her hand and kissed it. Several people glanced round, and she blushed.

'Why did you do that?'

He smiled whimsically. 'I did it for several reasons. Mainly, because I wanted to. But also because I've just left the darkness behind me. And it's such a beautiful morning.'

PORTRAIT OF A GREAT PAINTER

Anna Mary Robertson Moses' immensely successful career as an artist spanned twenty-two years. Her paintings, mostly of happy rural scenes, hang in major museums, and she has been acclaimed by critics and the public alike. This may not sound extraordinary—except that Anna did not begin to paint until she reached the age of seventy-eight!

Born in 1860, she grew up near the town of Greenwich in upstate New York. At twenty-seven she married Thomas Moses, and they settled on a farm and began to raise a family.

Thomas died in 1927, but Anna kept busy—running the farm, sewing and doing embroidery. As she grew older she developed painful arthritis, and her sister suggested she try painting as a pastime.

Her first pictures were copies of scenes depicted on Christmas cards, which Anna exhibited at country fairs. A visiting New York City antique dealer discovered her work in a local drugstore and introduced her to a gallery owner. Before long Anna had her first show: "What a Farm Wife Painted." A reporter called her Grandma Moses and the name stuck.

Mostly she painted "old-timey things," pictures Anna saw as dreams of the past. But in spite of her success, she was always first and foremost a down-to-earth farm wife. When she was entertained at the White House by President Truman, they didn't talk politics—"We talked plowin'."

On her ninetieth birthday Grandma Moses promised she would dance a jig on her hundredth, and she lived to keep that promise. Shortly before she died, at 101, she said, "I look back on my life as a good day's work. It was done and I feel satisfied."